# "You Want To Pretend You Haven't Thought About Making Love With Me?"

Dixie demanded.

"No," Flynn choked out, "but—well, I mean—"

"Is it *my* problem that your imagination is out of control?"

"I only meant—"

"I know what you meant!" Dixie thundered. "And it's the fault of men like you who want to pigeonhole women like me for the way we look—not once thinking that we might be doing the same thing with you!"

*"What?"*

"Do you deny thinking about me as a sex object?"

"Hold on! *You* kissed *me*, remember? Nobody kisses somebody the way you kissed me in the street today without deliberately planting the idea of—"

"That was different."

*"Different?"*

"You asked for it!"

Dear Reader,

As always, I am proud to be bringing you the very best that romance has to offer—starting with an absolutely wonderful *Man of the Month* from Annette Broadrick called *Mysterious Mountain Man*. A book from Annette is always a real treat, and I know this story—her fortieth for Silhouette—will satisfy her fans and gain her new ones!

As readers, you've told me that you *love* miniseries, and you'll find some of the best series right here at Silhouette Desire. This month we have *The Cop and the Chorus Girl,* the second book in Nancy Martin's delightful *Opposites Attract* series, and *Dream Wedding,* the next book in Pamela Macaluso's *Just Married* series.

For those who like a touch of the supernatural, look for Linda Turner's *Heaven Can't Wait.* Lass Small's many fans will be excited about her latest, *Impulse.* And Kelly Jamison brings us a tender tale about a woman who returns to her hometown to confront her child's father in *Forsaken Father.*

Don't miss any of these great love stories!

Lucia Macro,
Senior Editor

Please address questions and book requests to:
Silhouette Reader Service
U.S.: 3010 Walden Ave., P.O. Box 1325, Buffalo, NY 14269
Canadian: P.O. Box 609, Fort Erie, Ont. L2A 5X3

# NANCY MARTIN
## THE COP AND THE CHORUS GIRL

SILHOUETTE *Desire*®
Published by Silhouette Books
America's Publisher of Contemporary Romance

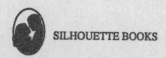 SILHOUETTE BOOKS

ISBN 0-373-05927-2

THE COP AND THE CHORUS GIRL

## NANCY MARTIN

has lived in a succession of small towns in Pennsylvania, though she loves to travel to find locations for romance in larger cities—in this country and abroad. Now she lives with her husband and two daughters in a house they've restored and are constantly tinkering with.

If Nancy's not sitting at her word processor with a stack of records on the stereo, you might find her cavorting with her children, skiing with her husband or relaxing by the pool. She loves writing romance and has also written as Elissa Curry.

# One

"Every cabdriver in New York must think he's a jet pilot," muttered Patrick Flynn, after swerving his vintage Harley-Davidson to avoid the taxi that came roaring onto Fifth Avenue like a guided missile. "Hey, buddy," he shouted at the driver, "you tryin' to kill me?"

But it was Flynn who intended to commit murder if anyone so much as scratched his precious motorcycle. He'd spent four years rebuilding this beauty in the living room of his West Side apartment, and he didn't plan on seeing his labor of love get the slightest bump on her maiden voyage around the streets of Manhattan.

"Take it easy, will ya?" he bellowed after the cab.

"Aw, take the bus, pal!"

Grumbling about the deterioration of mankind's appreciation for quality machinery, Flynn pulled over to the curb and let the rest of the traffic thunder by. It was at that moment that he thought he heard a distinct *ping* in the Harley's engine. Quickly, Flynn set both boots down on the pavement, then removed his helmet and leaned down to listen more carefully.

Or rather, he pretended to listen.

To any unsuspecting passerby, he probably looked like an average guy innocently listening to his motorcycle.

In reality, Flynn was a cop on surveillance. Within a two-block radius, he noted two additional plainclothesmen in a nondescript sedan, one more posing as a panhandler on the corner, and a woman pretending to window-shop across the street. Flynn feigned concern for his bike.

But the Harley's matchless engine purred in perfect synchronization, causing the frame of the bike to throb with delicious power just waiting to be tapped. Hiding a grin, Flynn decided that he'd never heard a more beautiful sound than a perfectly tuned motorcycle engine. The fact that *he* had tuned that machinery with his own loving hands—well, with a little help from his brother, Sean—gave Flynn enormous pleasure.

Then a scream shattered his perfect moment.

"What the—" Flynn looked up in time to see one hysterical woman fling herself out the doorway of a nearby church. She spun around and promptly began struggling to slam the massive oak doors closed behind herself.

"Help!" she cried. "Somebody help me!"

All the cops froze in horror. Here was an unexpected development.

"Help!"

She was dressed in a gaudy white bridal gown—complete with at least five pounds of pearls and a satin train that dragged behind her like the tail of a slightly drunken peacock. Her lace veil hung crookedly from—yes, it was a sparkly white cowboy hat. Flynn squinted to be sure he wasn't seeing things. A cowboy bride? She carried an armload of bluebonnets and staggered on a pair of white cowboy boots with pointed toes. New Yorkers get accustomed to seeing almost anything on the streets, but this was definitely something new to Flynn.

"Help!" she shouted again, much to the amazement of all the cops plus two passing joggers and one homeless woman pushing a wobbly shopping cart. "Please, somebody help!"

She looked like a country-western singer on her way to the Grand Ole Opry to marry an Elvis impersonator. Even for New York, she looked unusual. So nobody made a move to help the woman.

By herself, she managed to yank her massive train through the church doors, then slam them hard. Her veil tilted sideways, unleashing a haystack of long blond hair from beneath the Stetson. Then she flattened herself against the doors to keep them closed, breathing hard and shoving her hair aside. "For cryin' out loud, somebody *help* me!"

The joggers picked up their pace and ran away. All the cops pretended hearing loss.

With a frustrated howl, the bride threw down the flowers and hopped on one foot while yanking off one boot. She wedged the boot between the two door handles to hold the doors shut just as someone began pounding on the door from inside.

"Hey," the homeless woman called up the church steps. "Are you crazy, girl?"

"No," snapped the bride. "At least not as crazy as they *think* I am!"

With that, she left her boot between the door handles and hobbled hastily down the stone steps of the church. Snatching off her cowboy hat, she looked up and down the street and began to wave it frantically. "Taxi! Taxi! Why can't I ever get a cab in this godforsaken city?" she wailed. "*Taxi!* Hey, I— Oh, damnation!"

She laid eyes on Flynn and made a beeline in his direction. "What the hell are you?" she demanded. "An inner-city biker?"

"What the hell are *you?*" he retorted, not exactly coming up with brilliant repartee.

"Don't go asking a bunch of dumb Yankee questions," she ordered with exasperation, still hobbling with one boot on and one boot off. "Just get me out of here! And hurry! He's going to *kill* me!"

She had a gigantic mane of corn yellow hair and eyes bluer than a prairie sky. Her skin was milky white beneath a breathless blush, and her lips were a luscious shade of red. Too red, perhaps. And her breasts threatened to overflow her dress at any second. She looked like a riverboat gambler's shady lady encased in all that snug white satin. *Voluptuous* was a word that sprang to Flynn's momentarily stunned mind. Her eyelashes were like velvet, her earrings were huge globs of glittery rhinestone. Her wedding dress looked like a cartoonist's idea of a fairy-tale gown—all sparkly and poufed and exaggerated.

"You hearing me, sugar?" she demanded, hunkering down to glare straight into Flynn's face. "I'm runnin' for my life! Don't start cross-examining me like some kind of city-slicker lawyer, just help me, huh?"

Behind her the church doors burst open and six very large men in tight black tuxedos tumbled onto the steps, grunting and shouting at each other. One pointed at the runaway bride and yelled, "There she goes! Grab her, quick!"

The woman hitched up her voluminous dress, letting all New York glimpse a saloon showgirl's long legs, complete with red lace garters around her shapely thighs.

And a pistol tucked inside one of the garters.

She ripped the little gun out of its hiding place and pointed it directly at Flynn's nose. "You've just been elected my Knight in Shining Armor, sugar. So move over and let me on your horse!"

Flynn clenched his teeth and remained calm. "Forget it."

Her lovely mouth fell open. "I've got a gun!"

"I can see that."

"A gun means you have to do what I say!"

"I don't think so, lady."

She stared at him, and Flynn heard an emergency alarm start blaring inside his brain. In fact, his entire body was suddenly flooding with panic. It was crazy—*crazy*—to stand up to a gun-wielding nut like this! But he couldn't obey her. He couldn't. Not even with half-a-dozen goons bearing down on them like paratroopers storming the beach at Normandy. Every cop had to make a stand sometime, and this was Flynn's time.

Her beautiful face registered shock. "Listen, sugar, I'm gonna put a bullet through that thick head of yours if you don't help me right this minute!"

"Sorry. There's nothing you can do to make me get involved."

"Nothing, huh? We'll see about that!"

She grabbed the front of his black T-shirt with one hand and swooped close. Before Flynn could take a breath, she was suddenly kissing him.

*Kissing him!* Her full lips fastened on to his as if she were staking a claim, making her mark, claiming a prize. She was hot, wet, delicious, Flynn realized dimly. Sweet and spicy at the same time. Sexy and teasing and oh, so good. Her kiss packed a wallop of excitement.

For Flynn, time stopped. Talk about *crazy*. The city spun like a carousel and disappeared in a puff of sensual smoke. His whole world was suddenly this big, beautiful woman who smelled wonderful, tasted magical, and felt something like a wild animal as she pressed up against him. Jolted by a surge as powerful as any electrical current, Flynn felt all his strength drain away. He couldn't think, couldn't move.

And he didn't want to. It was magic. Black magic, maybe. Her kiss turned Flynn's insides to a cauldron of boiling hormones. He forgot his job, forgot his mission—hell, he even forgot his name.

Sex, he thought. The idea pierced him like an arrow. That's what he wanted. Now. With her. Let the kiss go on forever, prayed a voice he didn't recognize at first. Let their mouths melt together for eternity. Let their clothes evaporate, let their bodies meld into one hot, pulsing—

Just as suddenly as she'd started the whole thing, she pulled away and stared straight into Flynn's eyes with magnetic power. Her face was instantly carved into his mind forever. Those lashes, that pointed nose, those delicate brows. And that delicious, perfect mouth.

"Help me," she breathed.

Flynn didn't think. There wasn't time—there wasn't any need. He'd had one kiss and he wanted more. Lots more. Logic self-destructed. Common sense died a fiery death.

The men in tuxedos arrived in a puffing, sweaty pack, all grunting commands at each other. One of them grabbed the woman's arm. She cried out.

Flynn threw a punch—a lucky left-handed one. It connected with the man's chin and sent him sprawling on the sidewalk.

Another man—this one bigger and more determined—aimed a karate-style kick at Flynn's head. But he was far too slow. Flynn ducked instinctively, then seized the flying ankle and sent the man sailing backward. He landed on the curb with an explosive *"Ooof!"*

"My *hero!*"

Flynn slammed on his helmet and gunned the Harley as the woman gathered up her dress and climbed on sidesaddle behind him. Then he laid a patch of burned rubber on the pavement and they took off.

As they whipped into traffic, his passenger gave a whoop of triumph that sounded like *"Yii-ha!"* She tore the veil off her cowboy hat and threw it up into the air as they roared down Fifth Avenue. Taxis swerved, horns blared and pedestrians stopped to watch as Flynn opened the throttle and shot the Harley through an intersection with his passenger laughing and waving her hat with triumphant glee behind him.

"Use your spurs!" she cried, hugging him tight with one slender arm. "Oh, I've always had a hankering for men in black leather!"

"Are you insane?" Flynn demanded, shaken. His lips were still burning as they roared away from the church and cut up a side street.

"This is the sanest I've felt in weeks, sugar. How fast can this clunker go?"

"Clunker? This is a genuine— Why, I rebuilt this machine myself and I won't have anybody— Good God, put that gun away!"

"This little ol' peashooter? Honey, back in Texas we'd call this a toy!"

It was one of those miraculous Saturdays in May—not a cloud in the sky and New York's streets were newly washed of winter grime. Thousands of people were strolling on the sidewalks—now all pointing and shouting at Flynn's Harley, it seemed. He could hardly keep the bike moving in a straight line and it wobbled dangerously in traffic.

She leaned close. "Am I making you nervous, sugar?"

"Hell, yes, you're making me nervous!" *In more ways than one,* he wanted to add, not exactly sure of what had happened back there at the church. One kiss was turning him into a brainless mass of jelly.

"Whaddaya know," she mused with another whooping laugh. "An honest man!" She put her chin against his shoulder and snuggled close enough for her breath to tickle Flynn's ear. "Tell you what—I'll put away my peashooter if you promise to behave yourself."

"Behave my— What the hell is that supposed to mean?"

"Just do what I say." She waggled the pistol in front of him. "Promise?"

A sweat had broken out on Flynn's brow. "All right, all right! I promise."

"Good." She wriggled around, no doubt tucking the pistol back inside her garter. "Now," she commanded serenely, once the weapon was dispatched, "take me someplace safe."

"I have a feeling no place on earth is safe with you around," he retorted, meaning it.

She laughed delightedly and slid both arms around his waist. "That's what my daddy always said! You're a pretty perceptive guy, sugar—for a Yankee."

Flynn's perceptions were working overtime as she tightened her arms snugly around his waist and trailed one hand up his chest to balance herself. He could feel the curve of her breasts against his back, and the heady scent of her perfume filled his helmet in a dizzying cloud. Her body melded naturally with his as they took a corner.

What the hell was happening?

If Flynn hadn't been able to feel her body against his, he couldn't have been sure that she was real. Something had happened. Something amazing and somehow terrible. Flynn had never bolted out of a surveillance detail before. But here he was—acting like a maniac for one fantastic kiss.

Worse yet, he was contributing to a public spectacle!

Her trailing white gown and yellow hair whipping out from under her hat caused heads to turn up and down the street, but Flynn had to rely on his other senses to make a judgment about her. The Texas drawl and cowboy laugh sounded brash and cocky, but he thought he could feel the swift hammer of the woman's heart beating against his shoulder blade. And the tremble of her hand as she clasped Flynn's chest felt as if it was caused by something other than the shudder of the Harley's engine.

But she kept up her bluff, saying blithely, "You're in charge of this rescue, sugar, so go ahead and get me out of here!"

"Where do you want to go?" Flynn guided the bike up the street, half hoping she'd declare her desire to be nowhere but in the nearest bed with him. But his mind was beginning to function again, so he said, "The airport? Grand Central?"

"Heavens, no, there'd be a riot."

"A riot?"

"I have to go someplace quiet—where nobody recognizes me."

"Why? Who are you?"

"Why," she replied, sounding surprised, "I'm Dixie Davis."

"Who?"

She leaned closer for emphasis. "*Dixie Davis.* Sugar pie, if you haven't heard of me, you must be the only man in New York who hasn't drooled over my pictures in the tabloids!"

Flynn cut the Harley across a stream of oncoming traffic and pulled into the relative quiet of a tree-lined East Side street. He nosed the bike between a parked moving van and a city Dumpster before cutting the engine. Then he tore off his helmet and craned around to get a real look at his passenger.

She smiled, leaned back and lifted both arms like a chanteuse just arriving in the center-stage spotlight of a burlesque show. "Well?" she asked, blue eyes atwinkle. "See anything you recognize?"

Her low-cut gown revealed the perfect symmetry of her bosom, and no man alive could have mistaken that famous cleavage. Flynn peered closer at the equally curvy shape of her smile and the saucy light in her eyes, and he knew she was the genuine article. "I can't believe it," he said. "You're—"

"So it's finally sinking in?"

"You're—"

"Yes," she replied, lifting her nose to show off her famous profile. "Dixie Davis, who's taken New York by storm—a Texas Tornado, to be exact. Although I must say I'm disappointed it took you so long to recognize me. My publicist says I should be bigger than Marla Maples by now!"

It all made sense now.

Dixie Davis was the sexiest woman on earth. Even the *New York Times* said so.

Everything there was to know about the infamous Miss Davis had been screamed in giant headlines and suddenly here she was—perched on Flynn's motorcycle as happily as a rodeo rider on a pinto pony. In the past few weeks no red-blooded American male could pass a newsstand without seeing Miss Davis's exquisite figure posed on every front page. A month earlier she'd been an unknown dancer from some Podunk town in Texas. She'd blown into New York to dance in the chorus of a brainless Broadway show—*The Flatfoot and the Floozie*. But in a matter of days she'd been elevated to star status by the show's smitten producer—one of New York's most notorious mobsters, Joey Torrano.

And how could Joey Torrano avoid falling head over heels for Dixie? She wore sex appeal the way most women wore perfume. She was sexier than champagne, chocolate and satin sheets combined. Everything about her screamed *female* in big neon letters. Even the city's toughest, grouchiest columnists couldn't avoid writing about her.

The New York tabloids loved a sexy gold digger almost as much as they loved mob bosses. But this story had both—so Dixie had gotten press all over New York City. The so-so Broadway show looked as though it might become a megahit, thanks to all the publicity generated by a well-endowed showgirl.

"Dixie Davis," he murmured, wondering how many men on the planet would trade places with him in that moment just to get an up-close-and-personal look at the delectable Texas Tornado.

She was everything the press claimed she was and more. Her high-voltage kiss still burned in Flynn's memory. She was the real McCoy, all right—a blond bombshell who was part Marilyn Monroe and part Dolly Parton. An all-American sexpot with a heart of gold.

Flynn could only exhale. "Wow."

"That's me," she drawled, giving him her trademark sideways grin—a flirtatious half smile complete with batting eyelashes and an impish wink from beneath the brim of her white hat. At the same time she managed to flaunt her breasts with a practiced flounce. "Want my autograph, sugar?"

"No, thanks," Flynn responded. His senses were returning rapidly—as if plummeting to earth without a parachute. "But I *do* want you the hell off my bike!"

"Wh-what?"

"Pronto," Flynn added, climbing off the Harley. "I don't want to end up sleeping with the fishes just because you picked me to play Sir Galahad. So move your Texas buns and find a cab, lady."

"*What?* Your silly motorbike is more important than a human life?"

"It's not a motorbike—it's a Harley-Davidson! And I'm not risking my life for you."

She sat up straight, thunder on her brow. "Are you afraid?"

"You bet your boots I am! Your gangster boyfriend is Joey Torrano!"

"So?"

"So I assume he's the one you just left standing at the altar?"

"He wasn't standing. Not exactly, anyway." Primly, she said, "I knocked him down."

"You—"

Without meeting his agitated glare, Dixie Davis made a studied business of crossing one exquisite showgirl's leg across the other and wrapping the voluminous train of her dress over her arm. She began to swing her one bare foot expressively. "Well, I didn't have much choice, really. He was blocking the only way to get out of there! And I had to get away before it was too late."

"Correct me if I'm wrong," Flynn said testily, "but don't most brides wait until *after* the 'I do's' before running out of the church?"

"I decided I didn't want to marry anybody today."

Flynn tried to ignore the astonishing length of her creamy bare leg and the pretty arch of her bare foot. "But the groom disagreed?"

"Precisely. And Joey can be—well, very disagreeable when he disagrees."

"So I've heard."

"So I bolted like a calf out of the chute, sugar."

But Flynn thought he saw a flicker of dismay behind her brave smile. "Now what?"

"Now I'd like to go someplace quiet, please."

"I'll give you cab fare." Flynn dug into the pocket of his jeans.

"Cab fare! What kind of Sir Galahad are you?"

"The kind who plays it safe."

She flared like a Roman candle. "New York men! Honest to Pete, I don't know how you could be genetically related to our Texas fellas! Why, you're all a bunch of nervous old biddies—afraid to take a risk and never once thinking of a lady's feelings!''

She was a piece of work, all right—coquettish one minute and capable of lambasting him the next. A fire seemed to burn inside her. Was it possible that she was related to all the other women in the city? Those cool, well-dressed executives who marched the streets in their sneakers at lunchtime, each one looking much the same as the next? But Dixie Davis seemed so much more than anyone else. The gleam in her blue eyes filled Flynn with a powerful tingling sensation.

It had to be fear, he told himself. Here was a woman who could cause a hell of a lot of trouble.

"What's the matter?" she demanded. "Scared?"

"You would be, too, if you had any brains."

"You calling me dumb?"

"Let's be polite and call you impulsive."

Dixie Davis looked up into the frowning face of her rescuer and felt a wave of consternation. Maybe he was right. Lately her impulses seemed to be getting her into one jam after another. Seemed like she was snakebit.

Dixie's life hadn't made much sense to *her,* let alone to a perfect stranger. The past few weeks had turned into a kaleidoscope of events—confusing and exciting and sometimes downright out of control. First, there had been the audition and landing of a small part in *The Flatfoot and the Floozie.* Then she'd met Joey Torrano at a rehearsal and he'd seen stars right away.

After that, everything had happened faster than a DoveBar could melt on a Dallas sidewalk—but Dixie hadn't been calling the shots at all. She'd been swept up by Joey and the show, and—well, it had been so easy to shoot the rapids and enjoy the ride.

Until she found herself standing at the altar with a man she didn't even *like* very much.

"Maybe I am impulsive," she said musingly. "But I couldn't go through with the wedding. Not for the wrong reasons. I—I just felt like I better run away before things got any worse. You ever feel like that?"

He looked at her for a long moment. Something seemed to click in his head and then register on the narrow planes of his face. Then he said, "Yeah, I've felt like that."

"Now I don't know what to think," she said slowly. "I need some time."

"Well, we can't stay here," said Sir Galahad, suddenly acting as if he was waking from a dream. "The neighbors are beginning to suspect."

Dixie glanced upward and found several residents of the quiet street hanging out their second-floor windows to get a glimpse of her. One woman seemed to be talking on her portable telephone while pointing down at Dixie as if she'd just discovered Princess Di below her windowbox.

"Uh-oh," Dixie muttered. "In five minutes there'll be a dozen photographers here snapping my picture."

"And *mine*," said Galahad, slipping his helmet over his dark hair once more. "Let's split."

He climbed onto the bike and started it with a jouncing kick that sent Dixie grabbing for his waist. He turned his head. "Ready?"

"Ready!"

Dixie held on tightly this time as her rescuer guided his motorcycle around the streets, winding through traffic with smooth expertise.

*You haven't put yourself in another man's hands,* Dixie told herself sternly. *It just feels that way.*

She made a silent vow not to let this one take control of her life the way Joey had.

Of course, this one didn't act like Joey at all. He was younger—in his mid-thirties, no doubt—and had a sweet face beneath the hard expression he tried to maintain. He looked handsome and laconic—a young Gary Cooper. Only with more hair. She assumed he was some kind of mechanic, judging by his deep feelings for a silly machine.

Right off, Dixie had noticed a distinct gleam of compassion in his dark eyes. When she'd run out of the church, he'd been the only one to pay the slightest attention.

And he hadn't dumped her on the sidewalk when she'd begged for help. He'd even landed a pretty good punch on George's chin—George, who prided himself on being Joey Torrano's invincible bodyguard. He'd knocked George down without even thinking about it. The other bodyguard had been short work for Galahad, too.

He had good instincts, she decided. And a kind heart—even though he didn't really want one. For a simple mechanic, he seemed to be fighting a gentlemanly side. That thought gave Dixie courage.

She leaned forward. "One question, sugar. What's your name?"

Tilting his head back so the wind carried his voice better, he answered, "Flynn."

"Flynn what?"

"Just Flynn."

She laughed. "What kind of man gives himself just one name?"

"That's two questions," he retorted, demonstrating a modicum of humor.

"You keeping secrets, sugar?"

"Let me ask you a question first."

"Okay, shoot."

"Why did you kiss me?"

# Two
———

"**O**h, sugar, I *am* ashamed of that."

Dixie didn't want to explain. How could she, really? What sensible person would believe the power of the famous Butterfield kiss? It had started with Great-Grandma Butterfield and had been passed down through the generations directly to Dixie herself. All her life she'd been warned about abusing her gift. And now she'd gone and done it.

"I'm really sorry, sugar."

And she was. But Dixie had to know Flynn a whole lot better before she explained herself to him. He just wasn't going to understand yet. So she said, "Let's talk about that later, okay? Take me to the Plaza."

"The Plaza!" he echoed. "Are you out of your *mind?*"

"It's the safest place right now. Trust me."

"I thought you wanted to get away from Joey Torrano, not walk straight into his bedroom!"

"It's my bedroom, not his."

"You think that will stop him from sending his goons in to grab you?"

"Believe me, sugar, it's the best place for me right now."

He growled something deep in his throat, but opened the throttle and pointed his motorcycle in the direction of the Plaza Hotel, where Dixie had set up housekeeping.

She held on tight while Flynn wove his motorcycle through Manhattan's weekend traffic.

The hotel loomed elegantly over the southernmost edge of Central Park. A line of horse-drawn carriages drowsed in the sun out front, awaiting tourists. A liveried doorman stood on the staircase, frequently moving down to open the doors of the limousines and taxis that disgorged Plaza guests. He directed a fleet of scurrying bellhops to carry scads of expensive luggage in and out of the grand hotel.

All these sights had seemed like part of a movie set when Dixie had first arrived in the city. Now she accepted them as part of her amazing new life.

A life she couldn't wait to leave behind.

Since her earliest memory, Dixie had been groomed for her shot at the Big Time. She had taken tap-dancing lessons and endured hours at her aunt Lucy's Sweet Creek Hair Boutique. She'd entered beauty pageants and talent contests since the age of four. She'd been the Dairy Princess and the Fire Queen and Miss Teen Texas.

Now—finally—here she was in the Big Apple with spotlights and autograph seekers and a hit show on Broadway. People sent flowers and candy and marriage proposals.

And Dixie couldn't stand it.

*I'm going back to Texas as soon as I can,* she told herself.

But first there were a few loose ends to clean up.

Dixie clutched Flynn tightly when he swerved the bike across traffic to enter the Plaza. On the steps the doorman froze in his tracks as Flynn pulled his motorcycle under the hotel's expansive canopy and stopped. Flynn took one look at the disdainful doorman and made no move to get off the bike. Over his shoulder, he said to Dixie, "Look, this isn't exactly my kind of place."

"Not mine, either," Dixie retorted, clambering off the bike in a flounce of white satin. "But it's amazing how fast you can get used to luxury. Come on."

"What for?"

She faced Flynn, determined to hang on to him a little longer. For the first time since arriving in New York, Dixie felt as if she'd found somebody she didn't want to lose just yet.

Being honest for the first time in a long while, she said, "I need your help. You have to come inside."

Flynn looked stubborn. "Why?"

The hotel doorman marched over and sketched a bow. "Good afternoon, Miss Davis. We weren't expecting your return for a few hours."

"Oh, hello, Barney. Uh—I'm planning a surprise for Joey." She gave him a big grin and wound her arm sinuously around the doorman's burly elbow. "You'll play along with me, won't you?"

Barney responded with a blushing smile. He, too, had fallen for the charms Dixie just couldn't hide. "Of course, Miss Davis. I figured this was some kind of gag." He indicated Flynn's motorcycle with an unflattering wave of his hand. "You don't usually travel like this."

Flynn bristled at once and took off his helmet, as if readying for a fight. Quickly, Dixie intervened. "It's a gag, all right. Keep it under your hat, okay?" For good measure, she gave his doorman's cap a teasing flick with her manicured forefinger.

Barney gave her an adoring smile. "Okay, Miss Davis."

When Barney had strolled away with the air of a conquering hero, Dixie swung desperately on Flynn once again. "Come in with me for a few minutes. Please?"

He glowered after the doorman. "Listen, Miss Davis—"

"Please. I may need some help with my luggage or with the police, so—"

"Police?" he repeated, forgetting the doorman's insult. He frowned at Dixie.

She felt herself blushing. "Oh, don't go being afraid of a little ol' posse! They've been trying to get into my suite for weeks, and I just don't feel like fending them off by myself anymore. You could just stand in the doorway and look dangerous, couldn't you, sugar?"

He hesitated. "What are the police looking for?"

"Incriminating evidence, I suppose." Dixie sighed in exasperation. "Joey isn't exactly an angel, you know, so they've been trying to weasel their way into my bunkhouse for weeks. Oh, come on. It will only take a few minutes, sugar. Can't you play Galahad just a little longer?"

He considered the situation for another moment. He seemed to wrestle with his thoughts, then said almost unwillingly, "All right. A few minutes, that's all."

"Wonderful!"

Impulsively, Dixie gave him a quick kiss on the cheek. She couldn't help herself. He was adorable, really. Dixie knew she shouldn't be passing out those potent Butterfield kisses right and left, but she couldn't resist. For the first time since hitting New York, she found herself with a man who really had some appeal. He was good-looking and delightfully wary of her flamboyant appearance.

He reacted to her kiss as if he'd been stung by a bee—a response that made Dixie laugh. "Sugar, I think you're trying too hard to be a tough guy!"

Her laughter flooded Flynn with irritation. He *liked* her kisses, damn her, but he suddenly had an inkling that something about Dixie Davis was a little dangerous.

She grabbed his hand. "Come on, sugar. My suite is upstairs."

Her touch was almost as electric as her kiss. "What about my bike?"

"What about it?"

"I can't leave her here."

She laughed again. "Her?"

Flynn's temper began to flare. "This is a valuable piece of machinery."

"I'm sure," she said, clearly not believing him for an instant. She turned and waved to summon the doorman again. "Barney will look after it. Especially if you tip him well. Barney!"

Flynn felt a moment's panic. "How much of a tip?"

"Joey usually gives him a hundred dollars."

Flynn choked. He had about twenty-two bucks in his pocket—a sum that was supposed to pay for lunch and gas for the Harley. "But—"

Too late. Dixie was already using her sweet talk on the overstuffed doorman—an older man whose ears turned bright red when Dixie leaned close and cajoled him to take special care of the Harley.

Moments later she grabbed Flynn's hand again and dragged him into the Plaza Hotel.

Of course, he'd been in fancy hotels before. Plenty of times. Not exactly as a paying guest, of course, but police work tended to take a cop into all sorts of places—both good and bad.

But he'd never entered the Plaza with the likes of Dixie Davis.

Everyone in the lobby stopped doing whatever they were doing to get an eyeful of the Texas Tornado. The bellman leaned out over his desk to call his hello. The reservation clerks actually looked up from their computers to wave cheerily at their most infamous guest. Tourists turned and gaped. Some applauded.

Bold as brass, Dixie laughed and tilted her hat, then waved to her admirers like a beauty queen sailing down Main Street on a parade float. She kept moving at a brisk sashay—mostly, Flynn noted, to dodge the horde of people who pressed forward for her autograph.

With Flynn in tow, she dived into the nearest key-operated elevator. Dixie used a special security key conjured from inside the bodice of her dress, then she hit a button and collapsed against the rear wall just as the doors closed on a pushing crowd of fans.

"Whew!" She took off her hat and fanned her face. "Is it like that everywhere you go?"

"Everywhere," she agreed. "Except when I'm not Dixie Davis."

"What?"

"You'll see," she said with a wink. The elevator whisked them upward, and in a matter of seconds Flynn found himself following Dixie out of the elevator, through double white doors and into a luxury suite big enough for the NBA play-offs. Creamy white furniture, white carpets and a subtle white-on-white wall-covering stretched all the way to the huge windows overlooking a spectacular view of Central Park.

And there were flowers everywhere—roses in graceful arrangements, a single bud here and there, all with cards from fans.

But the suite's primary form of decoration was a life-size poster of Dixie Davis herself—spangled and primped and posing like a cowgirl from Mars who had just landed in the land of the free and the home of the brave. Her red, white and blue costume barely covered her spectacular figure, and her white boots were tasseled and pom-pommed. Her blond hair was huge. She was holding a shiny silver pistol that appeared to be shooting fireworks. Standing smack-dab on the coffee table in the middle of the living room, the poster created an awesome kind of altar to a living sex goddess.

Dixie threw her Stetson onto a sofa. "Make yourself at home, sugar."

"Miss Davis—"

"Dixie, please. Let me change out of this getup and we'll talk, okay?"

"But—"

"And if anyone knocks on the door, don't let them in. Unless it's Maurice."

"Who's Maurice?"

"The concierge. He'll be here any minute, I'm sure."
She exited the living room and half closed the door. She
began to undress, Flynn judged by the sounds of
swishing satin, but she continued to talk through the
door by raising her voice. "Maurice is a worrier. Joey
told him he'd better keep me happy while I'm staying
here, and Maurice understood that to be some kind of
threat, so he's always panicking when I change my
plans. Poor Maurice will go ballistic when he realizes
I've run out on my wedding."

"It's not Maurice's fault."

"Of course not. But he's afraid of Joey, you see. I
can't imagine why. Joey's usually a teddy bear."

Flynn considered what he knew about Joey Torrano, and nothing in the mobster's past made the man
sound the least bit like a teddy bear. A grizzly bear,
perhaps—one with a streak of vengeance and a nasty
habit of making his employees disappear when they
knew too much.

"Make yourself at home," Dixie called from behind the half-closed door. "Sit down and relax. Or get
yourself a drink. I'll only be a minute."

Half to prevent himself wondering what Dixie Davis
looked like while undressing, Flynn strolled around the
suite to see what he could learn about its occupant.
After all, for weeks the cops had failed to get into the
suite to look for evidence that might help send Joey
Torrano to jail. Now here was Flynn—actually invited
into the perfect place to find something useful.

He studied the suite through narrowed eyes. A white grand piano stood in one corner, its surface scattered with sheet music covered with pencil notes. A skimpy black leotard had been abandoned over the back of a chair. Flynn picked it up without thinking, and studied the small scrap of fabric with a frown, wondering how it could possibly cover Dixie's voluptuous curves. On the floor at his feet, a pair of worn-looking tap shoes lay where they'd been kicked off.

Remembering why he'd agreed to come, Flynn carried the leotard with him as he looked around some more. A few books and magazines were stacked on a table, but they looked as if they'd been ignored by someone who spent every waking minute rehearsing. Using the remote control, he turned on the television and discovered that Dixie—or Joey—watched CNN instead of game shows or soap operas.

A kitchenette lay adjacent to the living room. A peek into the small refrigerator revealed half-empty cartons of Chinese takeout, a couple of containers of yogurt, some apples, carrots, and a six-pack of Mexican beer. From all the police files he'd read, Flynn knew that the mob boss's favorite drink was vodka. Clearly, the beer was for Dixie.

The beer kicked Flynn's imagination into overdrive again. His brain quickly concocted a scenario that included an undressed showgirl sharing a cold bottle with a very turned-on cop. Ever since her kiss, he'd been aroused. No woman had ever affected him like that before. Flynn wondered if all men reacted the same way to the Texas Tornado.

A tentative knock sounded at the suite's front door. Flynn slammed the refrigerator shut.

"Will you see who that is, sugar?" Dixie called from the other room. "I can't find my shirt!"

The thought of a topless Dixie answering the door sent Flynn hurrying to greet the visitor himself.

"Who is it?" he growled through the door.

"Maurice," squeaked a terrified voice. "Is Miss Davis available?"

Flynn opened the door and stepped back to permit the concierge to enter. He was a panic-stricken little fellow in a black suit who scuttled instead of walked, and he wrung his hands as he rushed into the suite.

"Oh, Miss Dixie, I'm terribly— Oh! Where is Miss Davis?"

"Getting changed," Flynn said shortly.

"Who are you?"

Flynn came up with a lie after a second's pause. "Her bodyguard."

That was a logical explanation to the concierge. "I see. Is Miss Davis all right?"

"I'll be out in a minute, Maurice!" she caroled from the bedroom.

Pinpointing her location, Maurice forgot about Flynn and hurried to the bedroom door. "Oh, Miss Davis, I'm terribly sorry the Honeymoon Suite isn't ready yet. We weren't expecting you for several more hours and—"

"Cool your tamales, Maurice."

The bedroom door opened, and another woman walked out into the suite.

She was even prettier than Dixie Davis—tall and slim, with laughing blue eyes and a wide, happy mouth. But she wasn't caked with makeup or dressed like a ride at Disneyland. Gone was the flamboyant showgirl. In her place arrived a fresh-faced young woman with an eye-popping figure and a sweet smile. Barefoot and wearing a pair of snug, faded jeans and a man's plain white T-shirt that was loose everywhere but across her generous breasts, she looked delectable and innocently young.

Her hair was blond and cut short in a face-framing pixie style that accentuated the sharpness of her chin and nose.

From one slender hand dangled an enormous blond wig.

Flynn blinked and realized the woman *was* Dixie Davis—but without her trademark haystack of hair, the gaudy clothes and the hooker's makeup. She tossed her wig onto the sofa beside her hat.

Flynn was speechless. Her transformation was amazing.

"Now, Maurice," she soothed, curling her arm around the concierge's trembling one. "Don't worry about a thing. I just came up with a plan to surprise Joey."

"A—a surprise?"

"Precisely. I hope I can count on you to help?"

"Well, I—I— It won't get me—or the hotel—into any trouble, will it?"

"Of course not!" She laughed sweetly. "Would I toss you into the pigpen, Maurice?"

"Not you, Miss Davis, but Mr. Torrano is—"

"Just leave Joey to me, Maurice." She patted his arm placatingly.

"Will you be moving to the Honeymoon Suite?" the concierge asked, still a little nervous.

Dixie bit her lip as if to hold back a flirtatious smile and shook her head. "Not yet. I'd like to stay in this suite without Joey knowing I'm here. For just a couple of days, you understand."

A smile broke across the concierge's perspiring face. "Oh, of course, Miss Davis!"

"You'll keep an eye peeped for Joey, right? I, er, don't want his surprise spoiled."

"I'll alert security immediately." The little man bent forward and bestowed a kiss on Dixie's hand. "You can count on the Plaza, Miss Davis."

A dimple popped on her cheek as she smiled. "That's wonderful, Maurice."

She ushered him to the door of the suite. "Now, don't worry about a thing. I'll be out of your hair quicker than an armadillo out of a sausage grinder, I promise!"

"You can stay as long as you like, Miss Davis."

"That's downright neighborly, Maurice, honey."

When the concierge was gone, Dixie leaned against the closed door and said with an amused sigh, "He'll change that tune as soon as Joey stops paying my bill."

Flynn folded his arms across his chest. "Miss Davis, I think you've got some explaining to do. I don't understand most of what's going on. Maybe it would be better if I just left."

"No! Please, don't go."

"I've got to get to work."

"Well, could you take a few days off from the garage?" she asked, heading for the kitchenette.

Flynn followed. "The garage?"

"Where you work on your motorbikes. Couldn't you take a little vacation?"

"What for?"

"I've got a proposition for you."

Flynn's imagination immediately came up with several possible propositions—all of them including scenarios that required the removal of clothing that casually clung to Dixie's curvaceous figure. Flynn had a good idea of what she would look like naked, but he wondered exactly what shade her nipples might be, what the texture of her skin would feel like, how her voice might sound softly whispering nonsense in his ear. He could feel his whole body tingle and harden at the thoughts that crowded into his mind.

Unaware of Flynn's nosedive into sexual fantasy, she opened the refrigerator and removed two apples. Calmly, she offered him one of the pieces of fruit. "I'd like you to stick around and help me."

He accepted the apple automatically, although he wasn't thinking about his stomach. "Doing what?"

"I heard you tell Maurice you were my bodyguard." She polished her apple on the belly of her T-shirt and regarded Flynn. "That was pretty quick thinking."

"I had to come up with something."

She bit into her apple and chewed, studying Flynn carefully. "Would you be interested in the job?"

"What job?"

"Guarding my body. So to speak, that is." She swallowed her bite of apple and headed for the living room in an easy saunter that showed how perfectly her jeans fit the curves of her hips and thighs. "I mean, I might be needing some protection. Nothing life threatening, but it would be nice knowing there was somebody around here if I needed a—well, a witness or something."

"You want somebody to beat up your boyfriend if he comes around," Flynn guessed.

"Heavens, no! Although I'm still amazed by the way you stopped George in his tracks." Dixie sat down on the sofa and folded her long legs Indian-style. "Joey's not a violent man. But sometimes he loses his temper."

"And then what happens?"

"He shouts a lot," she admitted, studying her apple. "I hate shouting, so I'd like to avoid him. I want somebody around for a few days while I take care of some business."

"What kind of business?"

"Theater stuff. Don't worry."

But Flynn *was* worried. As a cop he knew he'd never get a better chance to get the goods on Joey Torrano. The Organized Crime Unit had spent the past two years trying to dig up evidence to use against the nefarious mob boss, but nothing useful had landed in the laps of the police. Until now.

But looking at Dixie Davis as she sat on the sofa nibbling her apple and looking anything but prim, Flynn knew it would take a stronger man than himself to resist her charms long enough to locate some evidence against her mobster boyfriend.

She looked up, and her blue eyes seemed endlessly deep as she awaited Flynn's answer. Her bottom lip was moist from the apple. Her blond hair wisped delicately along her temples, and Flynn's fingers itched to brush it away from her brows. There he'd press light, nibbling kisses.

"What do you say?" she asked, interrupting his thoughts. "I could pay you—oh, a hundred dollars a day. Plus expenses if you don't like expensive restaurants. How about it?"

Flynn didn't trust his voice and cleared his throat before speaking. "You don't know anything about me."

She smiled. "I'm a quick judge of character."

"Quick doesn't mean good. Maybe I'm your worst enemy."

"I don't kiss my worst enemies," she said softly. "And they don't kiss me back the way you did."

Flynn's mouth went completely dry. "Miss Davis—"

"I have rules about men," she said quickly. "I don't let anybody get too close. I know what I look like—some kind of cheap call girl, right?"

"Not right now."

With a wry smile, she ruffled her short hair. "But most of the time I look like a hooker on parade. Believe me, I know. It's all an act, though. It's show business. But I've learned not to trust men, you see. When I'm all dolled up, I know what most guys are after. But you're different."

"Maybe not very different," Flynn said dryly, thinking about the erotic fantasies he'd already indulged in.

She laughed lightly. "Yes, different. When I saw you on your motorcycle, you had a look in your eye. Kind of faraway. But definitely trustworthy."

Flynn bristled. "Believe me, Miss Davis, I'm not a Boy Scout."

"Let's put it this way," she said hastily. "You looked safe. And you turned out to be the right man for the job today. Couldn't you stick with it a little longer?"

Flynn hesitated. "How long are we talking about?"

Her expression brightened. "A couple of days, that's all I need to clear up a few things. You could stay here and sleep on the sofa. Please?"

The sight of her ingenuous smile made Flynn's heart turn over. With her simple haircut and no makeup, she was even more appealing than the woman who'd kissed him in the street. This one was just as sexy, though. Just as beautiful. And she wore her heart on her sleeve.

He quelled the response that rose within him and said, "I have to make a phone call first. In private."

"Sure!" She bounded off the sofa and threw her arms around his shoulders. "Oh, Flynn, I really appreciate this!"

She felt fabulous in his arms—her body lithe and full, her perfume sweet and tantalizing. How could she avoid sensing how turned on he was by her? She brushed another quick, electrifying kiss on Flynn's cheek and sent a dizzying smile up at him.

"Thanks."

Then she hurried away to the bedroom and closed the door, leaving Flynn stunned and shaken. He waited until his blood pressure returned to normal before making contact with his superior officer.

Flynn telephoned Sergeant Dominick Kello, currently in charge of the Torrano investigation within the Organized Crime Unit of the N.Y.P.D. Flynn got through to the sergeant quickly and summarized his situation.

Sergeant Kello could hardly believe their good fortune. "This is the best break we've had in months!"

"I'm not so sure," Flynn began. "What if I jeopardize the case?"

"What case? We haven't got a case! Maybe you'll finally get something we can use!"

"But she seems pretty innocent to me—"

"This is great!" crowed the sergeant, not hearing a word Flynn was saying. He covered the receiver, no doubt jubilantly announcing the news to the rest of the squad room. Flynn could hear the excited cheers and catcalls of his fellow cops as they heard where he was. Then the sergeant came back on the line. "Stick as close as you can, Flynn. Be her bodyguard, her chauffeur, her frigging costume changer if you have to!"

"I think that would be a very bad idea."

"It's a damn brilliant idea! Why are you so uptight?"

"Because she's—"

Again the sergeant's voice cut across his. "Listen, Flynn. Do you have any idea how many guys would kill for this assignment? All you have to do is hang around a beautiful woman!"

*An extremely attractive woman,* Flynn thought, clenching his jaw. Did Sergeant Kello have any idea how difficult it might be to simply think straight in the presence of somebody as sexy as Dixie Davis?

"Just stay there," his boss commanded. "Do whatever you have to do to get us some information we can use to nail Torrano. Got that, Flynn? Whatever you have to do!"

# Three

----

Dixie emerged from her bedroom wearing her huge wig again, along with a pair of fire-engine red cowboy boots, her tight blue jeans and a mouth-watering T-shirt. She carried a slouchy canvas bag over her shoulder and twirled a pair of cactus-shaped sunglasses in one hand.

Flynn put down the newspaper he'd been pretending to read after snooping through her suite. He had told himself he'd better snoop to keep himself from peeking through her bedroom keyhole.

At once, he noticed she was ready to leave. "Where do you think you're going?"

"To the theater, of course."

He sat up straight. "The what?"

"I've got a show to do!"

Flynn scrambled up from the sofa. "What do you mean, a show? This was supposed to be your wedding day!"

"I'm the star of *The Flatfoot and the Floozie*," she reminded him simply. "I've got seven shows a week—including matinees on Wednesday and Sunday. Unless I'm dying, I have to go to the theater."

"But—but—" Flynn found himself sputtering with amazement. "I thought you wanted to hide from Joey Torrano! How can you do that on a Broadway stage?"

"That's your job," she said with a laugh. "You're my new bodyguard, remember?"

"You can't possibly—I don't believe—"

But Dixie whirled away from him in a flounce of blond wig. Flynn tailed her to the door, where she checked her appearance one more time in the gilded mirror that hung there. Her reflection was enough to take a strong man's breath away.

She tugged an imaginary stray eyelash straight, then met Flynn's goggling gaze in the mirror. She smiled. "Well, how do I look?"

"You're not exactly going to blend into the scenery while sneaking out of the hotel."

"Is that a compliment?" She headed for the door and seconds later stepped into the elevator.

"A statement of fact." Flynn got in the elevator, too. "You're not the kind of woman anyone can ignore."

"Thanks—I think. But don't worry. I've got a cab waiting in the alley outside the hotel kitchen. Nobody will see me leave. Will you come along?"

"That's my new job, right?"

"Yes—if you still want it."

"I just don't think running around the city is a very good idea."

"People are counting on me. Tonight's performance is sold out."

"Don't you have an understudy?"

"I *am* the understudy," she reminded him. "Joey replaced the original star with me. We haven't had time to train somebody else. I have to go on."

"This seems like a crazy way to avoid the man you stood up at the church today."

"I know I can't avoid him forever. But I'm going to try until I can get a few things settled at the theater." As the elevator cruised to a stop in the basement, she shouldered her canvas bag again. "Ready?"

The elevator swished open, depositing Dixie and Flynn in the midst of the hotel's vast, bustling kitchen. The white-coated staff was deeply involved in preparing for the dinner hour, so hardly anyone looked up from their work to take notice of the two strangers slipping through their midst. But just as they neared the door, a shout went up and suddenly the whole kitchen was asking for autographs and pressing close.

Flynn fended off the mob and let Dixie slip out the door. She waved and called hello to everyone, but moments later Dixie was sliding across the back seat of a waiting taxi. Flynn climbed in after her.

"Hiya, Jerry," Dixie greeted the driver. "Thanks for coming."

The pudgy man sitting at the wheel grinned over his shoulder. "I haven't missed a night yet, Miss Davis. And I don't intend to. Who's the cop?"

Flynn stiffened. If he wanted to get any useful information out of his sojourn with Dixie Davis, he was going to have to keep his true identity a secret.

But Dixie laughed at the driver. "He's no cop! This is my new bodyguard. Flynn, meet Jerry. Jerry's been driving me ever since I got to town. I have his private number, and I call him anytime I need a ride. I hate trying to catch cabs in this town! And Jerry's discreet."

Flynn nodded at Jerry, who gave him a suspicious stare in return. Jerry said, "I've lived in this city all my life. I know a cop when I see one."

"Don't be silly, Jerry! Flynn is a mechanic in a garage, right? Shall we go?"

The driver didn't argue further, but continued to shoot glares into the rearview mirror.

The taxi sped across town in record time and dropped Dixie at the stage door of the theater where *The Flatfoot and the Floozie* was playing.

They were admitted through the stage door by an elderly man who'd been reading a racing form. Dixie explained who Flynn was and why he should be allowed into the building.

"Mr. Torrano didn't say nothing about somebody named Flynn. I got my list right here." The guard held up a clipboard. "See? There's no cop listed here."

"Flynn isn't a cop! For heaven's sake, Dwayne, what gives you that idea? He's my bodyguard, that's all!"

"He looks like a cop," Dwayne said stubbornly.

And Dwayne looked like an ex-con to Flynn. They faced each other like a couple of wild animals who knew each other by instinct.

"He's not a cop." Dixie put her hand on the clipboard, forcing it back down onto the guard's desk. "Let's just forget the rules this once, Dwayne. Can't you do me a favor?"

The guard tried to glower at Dixie, but it was impossible to look at her for more than five seconds without grinning. Dwayne manfully fought back his inclination to admire her. "I'm supposed to do what Mr. Torrano says. He pays the bills around here."

"Money isn't everything, Dwayne." Dixie widened her irresistible smile. "Remember that white-lightning cough syrup I made when you had bronchitis last week? It did the trick, right?"

Dwayne wavered. "Well . . ."

"Flynn's harmless, Dwayne. Trust me."

The twinkle in her eyes coaxed a smile from Dwayne at last, and his resolve melted. With a reluctant smile, he waved them through. "All right, all right. Just for tonight."

"Thanks, Dwayne!"

Over his shoulder, Flynn cast a glance at Dwayne and found the old guard glaring at him from behind his desk. There was a look in his eyes that Flynn knew well. An ex-con, all right.

Dixie led the way through a labyrinth of hallways and staircases—dark, echoing passages that seemed to tunnel deeply under the theater. Flynn made a mental note to memorize the layout as soon as possible. A cop never knew when he would need a back door. He could hear an orchestra warming up in the distance. Two men carrying an extension ladder hurriedly brushed past them. They called hello to Dixie, and she answered cheerily, not noticing how they nearly dropped the ladder and stared after her with goo-goo eyes.

Her dressing room lay midway along a hall lined with other doors—all of them decorated with pinups, greeting cards, cartoons and tinfoil stars.

A girl wearing a faded bathrobe, orange hair and elaborate stage makeup poked her head out of one door. She took one look at Dixie and squealed. "Dixie! Thank heavens, you made it! Hey, everybody! Dixie's here!"

At once, all the doors flew open and Dixie was engulfed by a crowd of chattering, cheering people dressed in wild outfits or very little clothing at all. Flynn had no hope of rescuing Dixie from the mob. Fortunately they all seemed delighted to see her.

"Tell us everything!" gushed a young man in a lime green zoot suit.

"Oh, Dixie, I can't believe you made it!" A petite young woman hugged Dixie with all her strength. "Thank heavens, you came! We thought we might have to cancel tonight's show."

"The evening paper's got your picture—the whole story—everything!" A burly man with muttonchop whiskers and a handlebar mustache waved a newspaper over the heads of everyone.

"Dixie, Joey's going to kill you!"

"Is he going to close the show?"

"Who's this handsome hunk, Dixie? The one on the motorcycle who helped you escape the church?" The girl with orange hair smiled flirtatiously at Flynn. "His picture in the paper didn't do him justice. Hiya, good-lookin'."

Dixie quelled the voices with a cheerful shout. "Calm down! Take it easy, everybody! We've got a show to do. We'll talk about all this stuff after the curtain!"

"But—"

"She's right," commanded a man in work clothes. Flynn guessed he was the stage manager. He held up his wristwatch. "Places in one hour!"

"An hour!" Dixie yelped. "I've got to get ready!"

She dived into her dressing room and Flynn followed. The rest of the actors breathlessly scattered into their respective lairs to prepare for the show.

"Sit down anywhere," she told Flynn, moving quickly to her cluttered dressing table.

Dixie had a routine for everything at the theater. She considered it bad luck to deviate from her regular schedule. First order of business was to make her dressing room cozy enough to relax in.

Opening her shoulder bag, she began by unpacking. First came her extra wig, her tap shoes, her makeup bag. Then came all her framed photographs, which she proceeded to line up amid all the junk on her dressing table.

"Who's this?" Flynn asked, surprising her by coming over and picking up the first photo.

"My father." Dixie proudly removed the handsome walnut frame from Flynn's hand. She smiled at the portrait—a photo that caught the infamous "Downhome" Davis looking particularly dashing. The photographer had managed to catch his character perfectly—half Wild West sheriff and half elder statesman. "Papa's the mayor of Sweet Creek. Doesn't he look wonderful in that hat?"

"Um," said Flynn, apparently unimpressed by her father's sartorial splendor. He reached for the second picture frame. "Good Lord, who's this?"

The second photo was a professional picture of Dixie's mother, Darlene Butterfield Davis, taken two decades earlier. Dixie leaned close. "Why, Mama, of course! She still looks just as fabulous. You should see her in a swimsuit!"

"Wow." Flynn seemed mesmerized by the astonishing length of leg, the thrust of bosom, the wide grin of Dixie's mother. Her satin evening gown managed to gleam on the curves of her hips. Most men had found Darlene Butterfield Davis irresistible. Apparently Flynn wasn't immune to her charms, either.

"Doesn't she look great? Mama was Miss Texas two years running! Nobody's ever done that but her. She won't say what years, of course. She's sensitive about her age."

"She's very...pretty."

"Pretty! She's drop-dead gorgeous!"

"I can see where you got your, uh, your—"

"The famous Butterfield boobs? I know. They're a blessing and a curse. My granny Butterfield was in the Ziegfeld Follies and became one of the first topless dancers in Texas. She got herself arrested four times. Mama always said topless was tacky, so I've never done it. It does seem pretty silly, don't you think? Waving your chest around?"

Flynn was seized by a coughing spasm.

Dixie patted him on the back. "Mama got me started in show business."

"She must be, er, proud of you."

"I hope so. I have to do the Butterfield boobs proud, don't I?"

Flynn coughed again, but controlled it this time. He reached for the last two photos. "And who are these guys?"

"Oh, they're my—"

She didn't get a chance to finish. The telephone by her mirror rang once. Dixie jumped, startled, but made no move to answer the phone.

"What's the matter?" Flynn asked, instantly on guard.

"It's Joey," she replied, staring at the phone as if it might jump up and bite her. "He always calls before the show."

"Don't answer," Flynn ordered. "I'll get it."

"Wait, Flynn. I'm not ready yet—"

He picked up the receiver on the third ring.

Flynn wasn't sure what to expect. But he hated the look of panic on Dixie's face. "Hello?"

A long pause. Then a gruff voice rasped, "Put Dixie on."

The voice was full of disdain, full of arrogance.

"Sorry," Flynn said, sure he had the infamous Joey Torrano on the line. "You've got the wrong number."

"Listen, whoever you are," the voice snarled. "This is Torrano. Put that ditzy broad on the phone right now."

Flynn hated the voice at once. He hated the contempt that dripped from every word. "Sorry, but you've got—"

"Let me talk to her now," Torrano ordered. "Or I'll come down there and—"

Flynn hung up before the threat was finished.

The phone started to ring again almost immediately.

"Don't answer it," Dixie begged. "I don't have time to get upset right now."

"You're the boss," Flynn replied, absurdly glad she didn't want to talk to the mobster. He waited until the caller gave up and then turned to Dixie. "Now what?"

"I have to get ready for Sven."

"What's a Sven?"

"Not a what. Who. He's the masseur Joey hired for me. He'll be here any—oh, that's him now." A short knock had sounded on the door and Dixie scooted to open it. "Hi, Sven, honey. Come on in!"

The already small dressing room was invaded by a huge young man who looked like a professional wrestler. In addition to a bright yellow headband that contained a spiked blond mohawk, he wore a clingy Gold's Gym T-shirt that showed off the glistening ripples of his chest and arm muscles. Skintight bicycle shorts clung to his massive thighs. He carried a portable massage table effortlessly under one bulging arm.

"Ready, Dixie?"

"Sure. Just give me a minute. Sven, this is my new bodyguard, Flynn. He's going to look after me for a little while."

Sven gave Flynn a long, measuring look. "Hi."

Flynn couldn't begin to guess the message in Sven's humorless eyes. "Uh, hello."

"Set up your table, Sven. I'll get undressed. Flynn, would you be so kind—"

Flynn heard the word "undressed" and forgot about trying to figure out Sven. He knew he'd better escape the confines of the dressing room before he was inexorably trapped with a naked Dixie—a fate worse than death if he had to keep his hands to himself.

But he found his path blocked by Sven, who unfolded his table and plunked it directly in Flynn's way. "He can stay," Sven ordered, eyeing Flynn with a stony glitter in his gaze.

"Maybe I'd better wait outside until—"

"No, put on the music," Dixie said, blithely peeling off her T-shirt. "See that pile of tapes on my dressing table?"

Flynn had never spent any time in the company of show business people. In the hallway, he had already noticed how casual the other actors seemed to be about their bodies. Half-dressed seemed good enough for them, and Dixie soon proved to be equally unconcerned about displaying her figure. She took off her shirt and tossed it onto the dressing table.

Flynn didn't have time to ogle the way her generous breasts strained at the flimsy lace of her bra before she kicked off her boots and reached for the zipper on her jeans.

Flynn spun around and pretended to search for the music she wanted. His hands fumbled through a pile of cassette tapes that was partially hidden under the huge mound of Dixie's extra wig. He knocked over a perfume atomizer and got a pair of silky pink panties tangled around his thumb.

"Find something suitable," Dixie suggested.

Suitable for what? Flynn wondered. Torture? He turned to ask, but realized Dixie was climbing onto

Sven's massage table in no more than panties and bra. As she lay facedown, she unfastened the bra and let it fall to the floor.

Flynn found himself staring at the most beautiful backside in the civilized world. The smooth shape of Dixie's white back blended into a luscious dip just above the twin perfection of her buttocks that were barely covered by her powder blue panties. Suddenly Flynn couldn't breathe. A sun-ripened peach hanging on the warm branches of a fruit-laden tree couldn't have looked more delicious than her bottom at that moment.

Sven took a bottle of oil from the dressing table and proceeded to squirt a generous amount onto his large hands. His huge body blocked the door, and he watched Flynn suspiciously.

Flynn tried to tear his gaze from Dixie and held back a groan. He realized he was trapped in the dressing room with a near-naked Texas Tornado—and he was about to experience the worst agony any man could possibly endure.

Watching someone *else* massage her body.

Overheated already, he took off his leather jacket.

"Plug in a tape," Dixie suggested from her prone position on the massage table. "Something soft and sexy, okay, Flynn? I need to get into the right mood for the show."

Flynn didn't bother to look through the collection of cassette tapes. He wasn't sure he was capable of reading at that moment anyway. He simply grabbed a tape and tried to plug it into the machine. As he fumbled with the tape player, he stared at Dixie's lithe body. Sven used a white towel the size of a dinner napkin to cover the curve of her bottom.

She wriggled out of her panties, dropped them on the floor, then stretched to get comfortable. Flynn's mouth went very dry. She was completely naked under that postage stamp of a towel.

Then Sven put his hands on her back and began to rub the warm oil into Dixie's skin. The music started and the small room was soon filled with the sensuous sounds of a soft guitar accompanying the husky voice of a woman Flynn did not recognize. She seemed to be singing in French.

Dixie gave a quiet, satisfied moan. "Oh, Sven. You're the best."

Sven didn't respond. He had his eyes closed and seemed to be lost in his job.

And what a job!

Hypnotized, Flynn watched Sven's hands smooth gently along Dixie's muscles. He could actually see her body relax beneath Sven's expert massage. He circled each muscle group in her back, isolated one after the other, and stretched them until Dixie sighed with pleasure.

Flynn wanted to strangle Sven for making her sigh like that.

He began to imagine his own hands performing the task. As Sven progressed up her spine, Flynn could almost feel each delicate knob of bone, each satinlike inch of skin. The oil melted on her flesh. Sven's hands were graceful as they stroked her supple shoulders and rubbed the tension from her slim arms.

Then Sven started down her back again.

Dixie murmured, "Wonderful. Would you turn the lights down, Flynn?"

Still staring at her, Flynn stumbled backward, groping along the wall until his hand connected with the light switch. He fumbled with it, then finally managed to shut off all the lights except a single bulb that cast warm shadows along the slender length of Dixie's back.

Then Sven hooked his thumbs under the towel and pulled it down over Dixie's bottom. His hands kneaded her there, leaving a slick trail of oil on her glowing skin. As Flynn watched, a large droplet of oil slowly, slowly disappeared between her buttocks.

Flynn bit down a groan of desire. He wanted to chase that droplet with his own fingers. He wanted to fill his hands with the soft flesh of her bottom. He wanted to shove Sven aside and caress her himself.

Most of all, he wanted to turn Dixie onto her back so he could feast his hands and eyes on the other side of her body. He longed to see her breasts, to touch them. He wanted to stroke her belly and find all the soft, most sensitive spots on her skin.

Sounding drowsy, Dixie asked, "Did you say something, Flynn?"

"N-no." His voice was little more than a rasp. To steady himself, Flynn leaned back against her dressing table. He could see her face from that angle, and a dreamy smile played on her lips.

He wasn't sure how much more he could stand. Every fiber of his own body was tight with urgency. With every muscle that loosened on Dixie's frame, another grew unbearably taut on Flynn's.

Sven worked silently, his hands dancing fluidly down Dixie's thighs, her sleek calf muscles, and finally to her feet. He paid careful attention to the arch of each foot and all her toes. Flynn thought about hurling Sven out the door.

Dixie seemed lost in a haze of sensual pleasure.

"Enough?" Sven murmured at last.

"Oh, yes," she sighed, sounding satisfied. "Yes, Sven. You'd better wake me up now."

"You got it," said the young man.

He quickly began to revive Dixie with a brisk rubdown that brought a pink glow to her skin. He was surprisingly rough with her, but Dixie seemed to awaken refreshed and energized. She made a wisecrack, and Sven laughed.

They traded jokes for a few minutes, but Flynn didn't listen. He was burning with jealousy.

"Lights," Sven said at last, jolting Flynn out of his fog.

"Oh, uh, sure." Flynn hit the switch and blinked unsteadily.

Sven handed Dixie a larger towel, and she sat up, neatly wrapping it around herself with the air of a modest Southern belle who wouldn't dream of indulging in such sensual pleasures as the woman who had moaned on the table just moments before. Her face shone with vitality. Her eyes danced with energy as she caught Flynn's gaze.

"You okay?" she asked.

"I'm fine," he answered hastily, aware that Sven was watching, too.

"You're sweating," Dixie observed.

"It's hot in here!"

"Is it?" She seemed surprised. "Do you think it's hot, Sven?"

"I'm always hot," Sven said with a grin.

Dixie laughed. "Well, open the door, Flynn, while I take a fast shower."

"A shower?"

Flynn hadn't noticed the connecting bathroom, which Dixie appeared to share with an adjoining dressing room. She slipped into the bath and flipped on the shower while Sven proceeded to wipe the oil from his hands with the small towel. Then he packed up his equipment.

When Dixie disappeared into the shower, Flynn ventured to use his voice. "How often do you come here, Sven?"

"I do Dixie before every performance," Sven answered. Apparently, Flynn had passed some kind of test, because the masseur began to talk in a friendly fashion. "Every actor needs to prepare before a show, and this is her way. There are a couple of actors I do after the performances, too."

"Nice work if you can get it."

"Oh, yes, I love my job. I work at all the theaters on Broadway."

"You must get to meet a lot of, er, interesting people."

"Lots of stars, yes. Dixie's the best, though. She's got a great body and a big heart." Leaning forward as if to share a secret, Sven said, "She's got the best butt in town, too, but she hasn't let it go to her head."

Flynn laughed, but wasn't sure if Sven was serious or not.

Dixie emerged from the shower then, quickly rubbing her skin dry and singing happily to herself. "Are you bragging about my behind again, Sven?"

"I tell everybody about your butt, honey. Your garbanzos can't get all the attention."

"Well, they say any publicity is good publicity," she retorted, laughing. "Thanks, Sven. You're just what I needed after a day like today!"

"Shall I come back later?"

"No, I'll find another way to wind down after the show."

Sven winked. "Don't do anything I wouldn't do!"

With more laughter, they said their goodbyes and Sven departed with his table.

Dixie turned her amused gaze on Flynn. "Well, that's the best mood I've ever seen him in! Sven certainly took a shine to you!"

"What?"

"He thought you were pretty sexy."

Baffled, Flynn said, "I don't—what do you mean?"

"He's gay, of course. Couldn't you tell?"

"Hell, no! How am I supposed to know?"

"Don't get flustered. It's a compliment."

"I'm not flustered!"

From the hallway someone shouted, "Thirty minutes till curtain!"

The message galvanized Dixie, and she forgot about Sven. "I've got to warm up now."

Flynn's head spun. Being with Dixie Davis was like keeping company with a tornado, all right. "Do you want me to wait outside?"

"No need for that."

In her towel, she began to hustle around the dressing room, arranging clothing, choosing another cassette tape, organizing her makeup. She plugged in a new tape and started to vocalize along with the recorded music. Through the half-open door, Flynn could hear other actors doing the same thing up and down the hall.

Dixie sat down at her dressing table, the towel slipping precariously around her otherwise naked body. She examined her face in the mirror. While exercising her voice, she began to apply her makeup. Her hands moved in quick, sure motions and she turned her face back and forth to catch the light after each layer of color went on.

Her voice grew stronger with every scale she sang, and Flynn liked listening to her. She had a good but not overpowering voice. There was an appealing sweetness to her singing. Other voices rose in similar patterns from the rest of the dressing rooms, causing the air to swell with cacophonous song.

Her face was quickly transformed into a vibrant mask of color. She applied her lip pencil last, then rubbed a bright red color onto her lips as a finishing touch.

"Fifteen minutes!" shouted the stage manager from the hall.

"Costume," Dixie said decisively. "Could you hand me that red thing, Flynn?"

"Red thing?"

"Right there." She pointed.

"This?" Flynn picked up a thin strip of elastic from which dangled a few rows of silk tassels. "It's not really a costume, is it?"

Dixie laughed at his expression. "In this show, it is!"

Her Roaring Twenties' flapper dress consisted of little more than a couple of feathers and the few rows of tassels that shimmered when she shook it.

"You're not going on stage in that?" Flynn asked, amazed.

"Why not? I look damn good in it!" She sailed into the bathroom once more to dress.

When she emerged a few minutes later, Flynn had to admit she did look good. Damn, *damn* good, in fact. The tight-fitting outfit managed to cover her with surprising good taste while still flaunting her figure to the max.

Involuntarily, Flynn whistled.

Dixie grinned and waggled her hips like a showgirl, clearly enjoying herself. She pulled on a pair of tap shoes.

"Five minutes!" bellowed the stage manager.

"Help me with my mike?" Dixie asked, handing him an electronic box about the size of a small transistor radio. She spun around and presented Flynn with her bare back. "Just clip it to the inside pocket of the dress."

Flynn hesitated.

He wasn't afraid to touch her. He just feared he might not be able to *stop* touching her.

"Problem?"

"No, no problem. No problem at all."

As delicately as he could, Flynn attached the microphone power pack to the lining of her dress.

"So far," Dixie asked over her shoulder, "how do you like this job?"

"Oh," Flynn replied, still dry in the mouth, "I'll get used to it."

# Four

Dixie enjoyed her share of the applause when the curtain was drawn at the end of the show, but she knew *The Flatfoot and the Floozie* was not exactly *War and Peace*. And her role, that of the floozie, was little more than a star turn. Eleanor Roosevelt could have played the part. All Dixie had to do was look great, flash her legs, sing a little and dance in place while everybody else showed off their talents around her. Basically, Dixie had to imitate her granny Butterfield—without taking off her clothes.

The show relied on the far greater singing and dancing skills of the other actors as well as the pyrotechnics that had become so important to Broadway shows in recent years. Still, Dixie got a big kick out of performing.

Unlike most of the cast, who dragged themselves downstairs in various stages of exhaustion, Dixie was bubbling over with energy after the show.

She grabbed Flynn backstage. "What did you think? Did you enjoy it? I thought it went great tonight!"

"It was good," Flynn replied, allowing her to drag him down the stairs. "You were terrific."

"I had a great time. Wasn't Kiki wonderful tonight? Come on. Now we have to go to the greenroom and talk to everybody. I called a cast meeting."

The whole cast of the show assembled in the theater's greenroom, a lounge where all the actors could relax. Some of the women slipped into bathrobes and drank directly from plastic bottles of mineral water to restore themselves after the strenuous singing and dancing. The men stripped down to their tights and wore towels around their necks to absorb sweat and the remains of their stage makeup.

Dixie entered the lounge with Flynn, who made himself invisible in a far corner. Dixie took center stage in the crowded room.

"Okay, Dixie," said Charles Kenton, the male lead of the play. He was the uniformed beat cop in the show—one who could sing and tap-dance like nobody's business. His powerful voice quelled the chatter in the room. "You've got to tell us everything now. Is Joey going to close the show or not?"

The whole cast looked at Dixie and held their collective breath.

"I'm not sure," she said in all honesty, hating to deliver bad news. She had never intended to become a leader among the cast members. The role had been forced on her. She'd decided early on to hold nothing back. Especially the truth. She said, "I think it's likely that Joey will withdraw his support of *The Flatfoot and the Floozie.*"

Her words drew groans from the cast.

"Come on, Dixie!" Charles blew up. "You've been in Joey Torrano's bed for weeks! Surely you could have used your influence!"

"I have *not* been in Joey's bed," Dixie snapped. "And everyone in this cast knows that's true."

Charles looked sullen while a few of Dixie's friends loudly stood up for her. The handsome leading man was a British native, and he had perfected a sulky upper-crust accent and attitude despite his Liverpool background. Few cast members actually liked Charles, but he was a good actor and dancer, so they tolerated his presence for a show that needed every asset it could get.

"Look," Dixie said, cutting across the raised voices. "You all know I was supposed to marry Joey today, and I didn't go through with it. I just—I couldn't do it."

"So now he's going to close the show," Charles snapped.

"It's not Dixie's responsibility to keep the show open," Kiki Barnes piped up. "We would've closed the first week if it hadn't been for her. We're lucky she came along!"

Charles kept his steely gaze trained on Dixie. "But you couldn't sleep with Joey to keep us going a little longer?"

"No, I couldn't," Dixie said just as coldly. "I've got my self-respect, Charles—"

"Not to mention two thousand dollars a week more than the rest of us for being in this show," Charles countered.

"I'm willing to give up that two thousand," Dixie retorted. "*And* the rest of my salary to keep the show open if Joey backs out. I'll do it as long as I can. But I can't do it myself, Charlie."

"Yeah," Kiki added. "If we want to keep the show open, we're going to have to find another investor."

"We can't let the show close," said another actor. "I need this job. And Kiki—well, she needs it real bad."

An odd moment of silence greeted that remark. Dixie knew perfectly well how badly Kiki Barnes needed her job in *The Flatfoot and the Floozie*. Kiki was providing financial support for her twin brother Kip, who was desperately ill with AIDS. Kiki's brother had been a dancer in New York for many years, and he was a good friend of many of the actors in the room at that moment. Nobody wanted to lose their job, for they all—Dixie included—pitched in to help with Kip's expenses, but mostly they didn't want Kiki to lose hers.

Working on the show not only gave Kiki money, but a reason to get out in the world every day.

Dixie planned to do anything in her power to keep the show alive as long as possible—not just for Kiki and Kip, but for all the people with similar stories.

"So." Charles broke the uncomfortable silence. "Where are we going to find another investor?"

"I have an idea," Dixie said slowly, causing heads to turn in her direction once again.

"Oh, yeah?"

"I think Joey might stick with the show if I left."

"No!" cried several voices.

"It's true," Dixie argued. "I've hurt his ego. He might keep putting his money into *Flatfoot* if I'm not around to remind him of—"

"Great idea," Charles said laconically. "But hardly foolproof. If you walk out, we're sure to close. At least with you on stage every night, we sell tickets."

"You haven't heard the rest of my plan," Dixie said. "I think we ought to challenge Joey."

"Challenge him?"

"Yes, by making him think there's an even bigger spender interested in backing the show. Then Joey might decide to keep his money in *Flatfoot* just to beat the other guy."

"What other guy?" Charles asked. "Where are we going to get another millionaire? Or have you found another potential husband, Dixie?"

Several of the actors turned to look at Flynn, who remained calm and silent. But Dixie flushed.

"No," she said. "I haven't found another husband or a millionaire. Maybe we don't need one."

"I don't get it."

"I mean," she continued carefully, "maybe we could make one up."

"What d'you mean?"

"I think Joey would keep his money in this show if he *thought* somebody else might beat him out of it. We just have to create a competitor, that's all."

"Create one?"

"Right." Growing more excited about her plan, Dixie said, "We have to tell the press there's another interested investor, and they'll do the rest."

Kiki had already warmed to the idea. "We'll need someone to stand in for pictures," she said, thinking. "The newspapers will want pictures."

"How about Charles?" someone suggested. "We could change his makeup, add a beard, put him in a nice suit for once—"

"No, the newspapers will see through that in a minute," Charles snapped. "I'm a well-known face. I'm famous, for God's sake! If this crackpot idea were going to work, we'd need a perfect stranger. Someone the papers have never seen before."

Everyone turned and looked at Flynn speculatively.

Flynn realized something was in the air and spoke at last. "What's everybody looking at?"

"He could be from out of town," Kiki said thoughtfully. "Florida, maybe. Or Las Vegas."

"California," said someone else, snapping his fingers. "He's too good-looking for Las Vegas."

"He'll need a story," said Charles, also eyeing Flynn with the expertise of an actor. "A background. Where did he get his money?"

"Oil wells?"

"Gambling?"

"How about professional sports?" suggested another voice. "He looks big enough to be a professional athlete."

"Flynn," Dixie said, "have you ever played any sports?"

"What's going on?" he asked. "What are you talking about?"

"In school," she went on, "did you ever play football or wrestle? Basketball, maybe?"

"I did a little boxing and—"

"Boxing!" Kiki crowed. "I love it! He's a former boxer with lots of money to sink into a Broadway show! Not only that—he's tall! Joey will hate him on sight!"

"Wait a minute," Flynn began.

"Here, try this on," said one of the extras. "This suit might fit you."

The group hustled Flynn out of his corner and paraded him into the middle of the room. Various articles of clothing were tossed in his direction, then someone dashed for the costume shop and someone else for the prop room. Dixie hid a smile. Her plan had been greeted with enthusiasm from everyone but poor Flynn.

He was pushed into several suit jackets until one was found that did fit him beautifully. It clung to his shoulders and tapered around his lean hips, looking quite stunning. A pipe looked silly in his hand, a cane even worse, but a fake cigar managed to transform Flynn into a believable character.

A mustache applied by the makeup artist completed the picture. Suddenly Flynn looked like a high roller with a shady past—exactly the kind of character the press might sink its teeth into.

"Hold on," Flynn protested as he was pushed and prodded by half-a-dozen enthusiastic actors. "I don't know what you're doing, but I can't—"

"Haven't you always wanted to be an actor?" Charles asked, finally siding with the idea but putting his own sarcastic spin on things. "Every man on earth wants to be a movie star! Well, here's your chance, Mr.—Flynn, is it? I don't suppose you can act, can you?"

Flynn returned to the Plaza with Dixie, totally opposed to the plan.

"I can't do this," he protested. "Nobody's going to believe I'm a professional boxer!"

"I'll coach you."

"All the coaching in the world won't help!"

"It's only for a few days," Dixie argued breezily as they entered her suite. "Long enough to convince Joey that he needs to sign an extended contract to support the show. Once we get his signature on paper, you're free!''

She flipped on a few lamps and tossed her canvas bag onto the sofa. Her wig followed, and she fluffed up her short hair with a brisk rub.

Flynn closed the door and followed her into the suite. He dropped a fake Louis Vuitton suitcase full of clothing the cast had collected for him out of the theater's costume shop. They had thrown themselves into creating a character for Flynn to play.

Desperately, Flynn said, ''Dixie, I can't do it!''

''Why not? You look the part! You look wonderful!''

''I feel like a fool.''

Flynn stopped and looked at his reflection in the mirror. It had taken only an hour for the transformation to take place, but he didn't look like himself anymore. Oh, maybe his own family would recognize him beneath the false mustache and the elegant Armani suit, but there was no doubt in Flynn's mind that his friends at the precinct wouldn't guess who he was. If they did, they'd bust their collective guts laughing.

Unmindful of his dilemma, Dixie kicked off her boots and started to make herself comfortable in the hotel suite. She yanked the tail of her T-shirt out of her jeans as if to undress right there in front of the windows overlooking Central Park.

"What are you doing?" Flynn asked, momentarily forgetting his problems. He wasn't prepared to start fighting his attraction to her all over again.

Dixie picked up the phone and began dialing purposefully. "I'm starving. I want to order some room service. What would you like for supper?"

"I don't feel like eating."

"Why not?"

"I don't know—stage fright or something!"

"That always wears off, trust me. Oh, hello, room service? This is Dixie again. Could you send up some— let's see—how about a couple of Western omelets? Oh, yes, with potatoes and everything. And some fruit. Oh, and something chocolate! Yes, that sounds perfect. For two, of course. Yes, for two people. Thanks."

She hung up and bounded for the bedroom. "You'll have to answer the door in your new getup. The hotel staff ought to get the first glimpse of my boxer with money."

"I thought you were going to keep your presence here a secret."

"Not anymore," she said from inside her bedroom. She didn't bother to close the door. "Now we're going to pretend I'm staying here with my new lover!"

Flynn shot to the bedroom door and halted on the threshold. "You're kidding, right?"

With her back turned to Flynn, Dixie whipped off her T-shirt and replaced it with a comfortable-looking man's dress shirt. She fastened a couple of buttons casually. "Of course I'm not kidding. The best way to make Joey furious is to pretend you've replaced him in my affections. Except for one thing.''

"Which is?''

"Joey never stayed here.''

"You never slept with him?'' Flynn said, not sure he should believe her. Unless Torrano was a man of steel, he *had* to have been attracted to Dixie.

"Of course I didn't sleep with him. I barely *knew* him! But we're going to make it look like you and I are—well, heavily involved. Trust me, it's the best way to get Joey's attention.''

Not to mention the attention of the police department. Flynn could almost hear his colleagues howling with delight over his predicament.

Dixie shimmied out of her jeans without revealing any skin. The large white shirt almost reached her knees and was actually quite modest when examined in a detached fashion. Flynn was anything but detached, however. She had great legs—slim and well muscled from hours of dancing, no doubt. And there was no hiding her famous bustline.

Unaware that Flynn couldn't keep his mind on the subject at hand, Dixie asked, "You don't mind staying here, do you? I'll make sure you're comfortable.''

*I doubt that's possible,* Flynn wanted to say.

"I'll even have your motorcycle brought up here if that would help.''

She gave him a winsome grin, and Flynn couldn't help smiling wryly in return. "It might,'' he said. *At least I'll have something else to think about.*

With a laugh, she bounded for the phone again. "Consider it done!"

While she telephoned the bellman to request the Harley, Flynn stripped off his Armani jacket and the expensive-looking tie he'd been given. He hoped the cast had packed a few casual clothes for his character to wear. Designer suits and ties weren't exactly his style.

He was plucking gingerly at his fake mustache when Dixie got off the phone.

"Oh, don't take that off yet!" she cried, coming over to pat it back into place. "You'll need it for the room service guy."

"Oh, come on—"

"No, no, I'm serious. He might be one of Joey's spies. Keep the mustache. It looks pretty good."

She lingered in front of Flynn, smiling up at him. "Very good, in fact."

"It itches," Flynn complained gruffly.

"Want me to scratch it, sugar?" Her blue eyes sparkled teasingly.

The moment lengthened. Flynn felt a tug inside his chest as he looked down into her face. She had scrubbed off all her makeup, and she looked wholesome again. She was downright beautiful.

But there was more. The cleverness in her face was clearly apparent to him. She was smart and talented. And Flynn had noticed how quick she was to give credit for *The Flatfoot and the Floozie*'s success to her fellow actors. But her presence had lit up the stage like no other. Still, she seemed not to notice. She wasn't the least bit self-absorbed.

An odd trait in a woman who could turn a man's insides to warm lava.

Her teasing smile began to fade as she sensed the change of mood.

"Um." Perhaps she noticed something starting to flicker in his eyes. "Maybe I'd better go take my bath. I usually take one after the show. It relaxes me, you see."

Flynn cleared his throat. "Don't let me stop you."

"Call me when supper gets here."

She slipped into the bathroom, and Flynn heard her turn on the water. He blew a sigh of relief.

It wasn't smart to be attracted to the woman you were supposed to be watching, Flynn knew. That was one of the first rules a cop had to learn. Sex always complicated things. Sometimes it screwed up legal cases until the bad guys stayed out of jail.

Sometimes it cost good cops their jobs.

Over the sound of running water, Flynn heard Dixie start to warble one of the songs from *The Flatfoot and the Floozie*. He wondered whether she had taken off all her clothes yet.

With a silent curse at his active imagination, Flynn made a beeline for the telephone. He probably had time to make a quick call to the precinct to get his mind back where it belonged.

But Sergeant Kello wasn't at his desk. He'd gone home for the night. Frustrated, Flynn hung up. He heard Dixie splashing water in the tub.

How had things gotten this far? He was supposed to be a cop on surveillance—nothing more. But somehow he was masquerading in a borrowed suit and wearing a ridiculous false mustache, to boot.

And the worst of it was obviously going to be spending the night in Dixie's suite. A terrible thought struck him, and Flynn stopped pacing. He wondered if she slept in the nude.

A soft knock at the suite's door announced the arrival of dinner. The waiter didn't seem to notice anything silly about Flynn's mustache. He seemed very curious about Flynn's presence in the suite, however, and he certainly heard Dixie singing in the bathtub—complete with splashing. If he was one of Torrano's spies, he was going to have plenty of stories to tell the boss later.

Just behind the waiter came the hotel's bellman, gingerly wheeling Flynn's Harley out of the elevator. Flynn forgot about food and leapt to take possession of his bike. Running his hands over the motorcycle, he checked for dents or scratches. It seemed to be in perfect condition.

"Nice bike," said the bellman, clearly trying to figure out who Flynn was.

Since he couldn't come up with a plausible reason why the mysterious ex-boxer from California would have a vintage Harley-Davidson in the city, Flynn said curtly, "Thanks," and sent the curious bellman on his way.

Alone again, Flynn parked his bike beside the white piano and wheeled the room-service cart into Dixie's plush bedroom.

"Is that our food?" Dixie called from the tub. "Or your motorcycle?"

"Both." Flynn checked under the lids of several dishes and called, "Food smells delicious!"

"And the motorcycle?" she called back, laughter in her voice.

"Perfect shape."

"Great. Bring the supper in here!"

Obediently, Flynn wheeled the cart through her cluttered bedroom to the doorway of the bathroom.

"Come on in," Dixie said. "I'm decent."

Cautiously, Flynn stuck his head around the door.

She was not decent.

At least, she probably wasn't. Dixie had filled the bathtub with steaming hot water and loaded it with bubbles. The water was still running, and the bubbles had risen high enough to cover her breasts. Just barely.

"I think I'll wait out here until you're dried off," Flynn said hastily.

"Don't be silly," she said. "I'm covered up. The food will get cold. Just wheel it in here and we'll eat. Come on. It's no big deal."

Flynn leaned against the doorframe and passed one hand through his hair. "For me, it's a big deal."

Dixie laughed. "In the theater, we get used to changing our clothes in front of fifty people backstage between scenes. If you hang around with us for more than a couple of days, you'll see what I mean."

"I've seen plenty already, thanks."

"Come on in. Really, I don't mind."

Flynn argued with himself for about thirty seconds. But he realized he'd like nothing better than having dinner while admiring Dixie Davis in her bath. Besides, he might actually learn more by interrogating her.

*What the hell, Flynn,* he said to himself. *How many perks does this job have? Not many, pal. Take advantage of this one while you can.* So he shrugged and pushed the cart into the warm bathroom. It was mostly marble and mirrors, with an enormous Jacuzzi and a huge window that overlooked Central Park.

Dixie had sunk down into the bubbles as far as her chin. "Now, won't this be cozy? Park the cart right here, sugar. And you can sit on the dressing table chair, see? I have some beer in the ice bucket over there. Have one."

She was sipping from a bottle herself. Three more bottles of Mexican beer were floating in a large ice bucket on the bathroom counter alongside an enormous display of makeup bottles, tubes and pencils. Flynn helped himself to a beer.

Dixie took a long swallow and relaxed into the tub with a sigh. "This tastes wonderful."

*You look wonderful,* Flynn almost said.

But he didn't. It wasn't the kind of thing a cop was supposed to say to the woman he was investigating—no matter how much he believed it.

Instead, Flynn silently handed her one of the steaming plates and a fork. She balanced her beer on the edge of the huge tub and accepted the plate eagerly.

"I'm famished!"

"You worked up an appetite tonight," Flynn remarked, sitting back on the brass and velvet dressing table chair, his own plate in hand. "I've never seen a Broadway show up close like that before. You people really get a workout."

"All that singing and dancing—you bet." Dixie dug into her omelet with gusto. "My granny Butterfield says she used to lose five pounds every night she did a show."

"Your grandmother was on Broadway?"

"I told you, she was a Ziegfeld Folly! And she was wonderful. I have some of her pictures in my suitcase if you'd—"

"It can wait," Flynn said, alarmed that she might try climbing out of the tub then and there to get the photographs.

"She was something! Of course, she's no slouch even now. She was Mama's coach at the Miss America pageant."

"You come from quite a family."

"Oh, yes, I've got show business all over Mama's side of the family. Granny Butterfield and all her sisters have given me a lot of pointers."

"I could use some pointers myself," Flynn murmured, digging into his food. It tasted surprisingly good, and he realized he was hungry indeed.

Dixie eyed him for a moment, chewing. "You're not such a bad actor, I'll bet," she said around a mouthful of home-fried potatoes. "It won't take much for Joey to believe you're a hotshot from California."

Flynn was amused. "I look like a hotshot?"

"A dangerous kind of hotshot, yes, when you've got a certain frown on. The only trouble is, your face doesn't look beaten up enough to pass for a boxer's."

"I draw the line at makeup," Flynn said quickly. "This damned mustache is bad enough."

"Here, we can take that off now."

Dixie slid over to the edge of the tub and put her plate aside. In that new position, her glistening bare back was reflected in the gigantic, half-steamed mirrors that lined the luxurious bathroom. She reached up one slender arm and Flynn obediently leaned down. His heart suddenly began to thump in his chest. Tentatively she tugged at the fake mustache on his upper lip, smiling.

"Ow." Flynn winced. "Take it easy."

"Are you a big baby, after all?" she teased.

"Hell, no, but this thing was put on with some kind of super glue that— *Yeow!*"

"There!" She held up the mustache triumphantly. "It's better to get it over with quickly. Now, eat your supper."

But suddenly Flynn felt much more like leaning down over the tub and inhaling the fragrant scent of the bathwater. He wanted to get a handful of those fluffy bubbles and smooth them down the graceful length of Dixie's moist arm.

He fought the impulse and tried to get his mind back on the business at hand. He had an interrogation to conduct.

"Er— Did you ever have dinner in the bathtub with Joey Torrano?"

Dixie forgot about eating for a moment and looked surprised. "Not exactly, no."

Flynn continued to eat, pretending not to care about her responses. "You must have spent a lot of time with the guy. I mean, to want to marry him."

"I didn't really want to marry him," she explained, idly playing her fork through her food. "I was—well, not forced, exactly. I don't know how it happened, to tell the truth. Joey was the producer of *The Flatfoot and the Floozie* and we spent a lot of time together at the theater. I could see that he was attracted to me. Most men are."

Flynn ground his teeth.

"Next thing I knew," Dixie continued, "well, I was walking down the aisle again."

"Again?" Flynn echoed.

Dixie smiled uncertainly. "I told you before—in show business a woman has to look after herself. So I follow my mama's rules. Rule Number One is, never make love with a man you're not married to."

"Never—"

"Right. Never go to bed with anyone but your husband."

"You mean—"

Dixie turned a lovely shade of pink. "Joey wanted to sleep with me, and I—I just couldn't do it. Not without benefit of marriage. I don't know why I'm such an old-fashioned prude, but I just can't—well, get excited about a man unless—"

"You mean," Flynn interrupted, astonished by what he was hearing from the sexiest woman alive. "You mean, you're a *virgin?*"

"Of course not," Dixie said blithely. "I've been married twice already. Joey was going to be my third husband."

"Your *third*—"

"I know, I'm hardly old enough, am I? But it's true. I don't sleep around. I marry."

"Do you skip the part about death do you part?"

She picked up her plate again, but didn't attack the food once more. Her gaze seemed faraway for a moment. "No, but I—my marriages didn't work out. That's very painful to me."

"I'm sorry."

"I decided not to make another mistake with Joey, no matter how good the cause—well, no matter what."

The telephone rang.

Dixie regained her good humor. "Could you hand me the phone, please? Under all these bubbles, I'm not exactly—"

"Right," said Flynn, abandoning his plate and reaching for the telephone among the clutter on the bathroom counter. Numbly, he passed the receiver to Dixie in the tub.

Dixie accepted the receiver. "Hello?"

She went pale and choked, pressing one hand over her throat as if to steady her pulse. "Joey?"

Flynn leaned toward her.

Dixie swallowed hard and said, "Yes, of course I did the show tonight. Why wouldn't I?"

Flynn put his hand over Dixie's on the edge of the tub and found that she was trembling.

Into the phone, she said, "I had to do the show, Joey. Everyone was counting on me. We had a sold-out theater."

She listened to Torrano lecture for a few seconds and finally said, "Joey, wait. Listen. I'm sorry. Really, I am. I just couldn't go through with it…. Yes, of course I know I embarrassed you, but I couldn't help it. I'm *sorry,*" she repeated.

"Hang up," Flynn whispered.

She looked at Flynn wide-eyed, but didn't hang up the receiver. "No, Joey," she said, suddenly pleading. "Please don't back out of the show on my account. Everyone's depending on you. And we really are selling tickets. The show will start turning a profit in a few months. It will be a great investment, I promise!"

Joey Torrano apparently did not believe her. He began a tirade that caused Dixie's jaw to tighten. Then she rolled her eyes impatiently.

She said more firmly, "Joey, you have to do whatever you think is right. If you have to back out of the show—well, maybe another investor will turn up."

This time Torrano began to scream into the telephone. Dixie smiled up at Flynn and winked. She covered the receiver and whispered, "You know, I think he might actually fall for this!"

"Don't push your luck," Flynn said, keeping his voice low. "Just hang up and let the press give him the message tomorrow. That's the way the plan is supposed to go."

She nodded, uncovered the receiver, and said, "I've got to go, Joey. Yes, I had dinner sent up and—no, of course there's nobody here with me. Why would you think that?"

Torrano shouted some more.

"No," Dixie said. "I'm quite alone at the moment, Joey. Now, you go to sleep and think about whether you want to sign a contract to support the show, okay? Yes, good night. Good *night*, Joey!"

She tossed the receiver to Flynn and whooped. "Wonderful! He's suspicious already!"

"Suspicious about what?"

"You!" Dixie exuberantly splashed water into the air. "He had one of his spies in the hotel tonight. The guy must have spotted you and reported to Joey." Delighted, she crowed, "They think I've got a man up here!"

"You do," Flynn observed.

# Five

----

"**W**ell, we'll let Joey get his trousers in a twist and see what happens." Dixie settled back into the bubbles, pleased with the way her plan was going.

Flynn looked less than pleased. "You're playing a dangerous game, Miss Davis."

"I don't play games."

"I think," he argued very carefully, "you play games all the time."

"I do not!"

"First the Texas Tornado act, and—"

"That may be an act," Dixie quickly conceded, "but it gets things accomplished."

"Isn't that a game?"

"It's business."

"Show business." Flynn nodded. "You manipulate people—first to entertain, then to make them give what you want."

"Are we talking about Joey now?" Dixie demanded. "Don't feel sorry for him. Joey got what he wanted out of our relationship, if that's what you mean."

"But you never slept with him."

"That's not what he wanted!" Dixie sat up defensively. "Oh, he thought I was sexy and all, but he wanted me so I'd make him look good!"

"It's pretty tough to make a lifetime criminal look good," Flynn snapped. "But you managed to do it."

"Only for the benefit of the newspapers," Dixie replied. She lifted her toes out of the bathwater to check her pedicure. "Anyway, Joey's not so bad."

"You don't think so?" Flynn's dark eyes were suddenly hard, and he seemed unaware of her dripping leg as she extended it in a leisurely stretch above the fragrant bubbles.

Dixie slipped her leg out of sight again. "He's given a lot of money to the show."

"Is money the way you measure goodness in people?"

"Of course not!"

"You seem to be protecting him."

"Maybe I am in a way. I just think—well, you have to know my friends, the ones who work with me at the theater. They're—they all have different stories—different reasons why the show is so important. I want to keep it going a little longer. I owe them that much."

"You owe them? Why?"

Dixie decided not to answer that one directly. "Look, I admit I'm not exactly what I seem—"

"You're not the Texas Tornado?"

"Yes, in a way. I mean, it's who I am—where I come from."

"But I notice you drop the drawl and the lingo when we're alone."

Suddenly she didn't like the laughter in his gaze. "Of course I play it up a little! Why, my mama and Granny Butterfield think they've died and gone to hog heaven—me on the legitimate Broadway stage and all—but I—oh, hell, my real name isn't even Dixie!"

"It isn't?"

"Daddy called me Dixie from the time I was knee-high to a longhorn steer, but my given name is..."

He noticed her reluctance at once. "Your given name is?"

She sighed. "Diana. Boring, huh?"

He sat forward on the velvet chair. "Not boring. Nice."

Suddenly Dixie felt awkward. She wasn't used to men who actually wanted to know her. Since coming to New York, she had been subjected to some of the most ham-handed wooing since her uncle Smokey had proposed to his first wife while teaching her the rudiments of silage.

"In my family," she said slowly, "boring is boring. You have to be a character or you fade into the woodwork. So I became Dixie—with some help from Granny Butterfield and Mama, that is. Between having Miss Texas and a fan dancer for tutors, and—well, this is what you get." She lifted her arms from the bath bubbles. "Ta-da!"

Flynn smiled, one brow raised wryly. "It's a pretty nice package, I must say. You've certainly knocked New York on its ear."

"The Sexiest Woman on Earth? Oh, that's nonsense!"

Flynn took a breath and let it out slowly, trying to fight down the feelings that were starting to bubble inside him again. It was hard watching her enjoy her bath. "You're the sexiest thing to come to this city in a long time."

She slid over to the edge of the tub again. "Do you think so?"

He couldn't help leaning closer, longing to take her lips with his to see if they melted like cotton candy. "I think everybody thinks so."

"Just because I have a sense of humor about my body? About sex?" Dixie shook her head, looking wise. She laid her forearms on the edge of the tub and floated on her belly. "Listen, this is the body I was born with, so what am I supposed to do? Hide it because big breasts are politically incorrect right now? Hell, I might as well have a laugh at my own expense and enjoy it!"

"Some women would say you're being exploited."

"Maybe some women who take their clothes off *are* exploited," she retorted. "But I take care of myself. I don't jump into bed with anyone who comes along. I don't do bump-and-grind stuff or humiliate myself. If sex can't be fun, it's—well, it feels dirty to me, you know?"

"You certainly look like you're having fun," Flynn agreed, trying hard to keep his eyes from traveling down the heaps of bubbles to get a glimpse of the body in question.

"I am having fun. I've got a life besides sex, though. Everybody assumes I'm thinking about bedrooms all the time because I look the way I look. But I have a real life!"

"Flaunting yourself onstage?"

"That's not why I'm here," she began. "I mean, I've got a job to do—"

"Acting like the new Marilyn Monroe?"

"No! Yes. Well, maybe. Look, underneath the Texas Tornado act, everything is really pretty innocent, don't you think?" Her blue gaze was direct and challenging as she looked at him from the mounds of perfumed bubbles.

Flynn didn't feel the least bit innocent at that moment. All he could think about was diving into the tub with her and covering her talkative mouth with his own.

"If you wanted to be innocent," Flynn said slowly, "you'd be wearing a nun's habit around town instead of that big white hat and a push-up bra."

"I do not wear push-up bras!" She sat up again.

"You know what I mean."

"No, I don't! Hand me that towel!" Her temper began to blaze. "I have a body that gives out messages maybe I don't necessarily want to broadcast to the world, but I can't help the way I look!"

"You could tone it down." Flynn pulled a fluffy white towel from the heated rack and passed it to Dixie.

"Why should I?" she demanded, snatching the towel from his grasp. "Am I supposed to be punished for having this figure?"

"No, but—"

"Should I be forced to wear uncomfortable clothes because of the way I look?"

"Well—"

"I hate being told what to do!"

"I'm not—"

"It's *you* who can't control what you're thinking," Dixie snapped, suddenly standing up and whipping the towel around herself. The mirrors behind her gave away all her secrets, and Flynn caught a beautiful glimpse of her naked bottom dripping suds and warm water.

The glare in Dixie's eyes was very hot, though. "You look at me and think about making love with this body, but is that my problem? No!"

"I didn't—"

"You want to pretend you haven't thought about sex with me?"

"No, but— Well, I mean—"

"Is it *my* problem that your imagination is out of control?"

"But—"

"Should I stifle who I am because of what's going on in *your* head?"

"I only meant—"

"I know what you meant!" Dixie thundered. "And it's the fault of men like you who want to pigeonhole women like me for the way we look—not once thinking that we might be doing the same thing with you!"

*"What?"*

She pulled herself up very straight and trembled with outrage. "I think you'd better leave, Mr. Flynn."

"Wait a minute—"

"Do you deny thinking about me as a sex object?"

"Hold on! *You* kissed *me*, remember? Nobody kisses somebody the way you kissed me in the street today without deliberately planting the idea of—"

"That was different."

*"Different?"*

"You asked for it!"

*"I* asked for—"

"It's time you left my bathroom, Flynn." She hugged her towel like a Victorian lady taking offense at the uncouth actions of a barbarian.

"Exactly what just happened here?" he demanded, a little drunk from just watching the bathwater stream down her exquisitely long and shapely legs.

"You can sleep on the sofa in the living room," she said tartly. "Good night."

"But—"

"I said, good night."

"I—"

*"Scram!"*

Flynn scrammed. When he'd closed the door and fled, he could hear Dixie slamming bottles and plates around the bathroom, having a temper tantrum.

On the sofa later, he tossed and turned, trying to figure out what he'd said or done that was wrong. But either Dixie's argument hadn't made any sense or his brains were truly scrambled by being so near her.

In the morning her bedside telephone woke Dixie bright and early. "Yes?"

"Good morning, sleepyhead!" chorused two voices on the phone. She recognized the high spirits of two friends from the theater—Rob and Jan Murdock, who were known as Rob and Jan Munchkin because they were both quite small and always adorable.

In Dixie's ear, Rob sang, "We're in the lobby—here to help make your boyfriend believable. Let us in!"

"He's not my boyfriend," Dixie grumbled, remembering her battle with Flynn the night before. She rubbed one eye and glowered at the alarm clock. It was almost ten, time to get up, anyway.

"Whatever," Rob said with a laugh. "Tell us the suite number and we'll be right up."

Dixie did so, then slid out of bed and headed for the bathroom. Minutes later she felt presentable and went out to wake Flynn before her friends arrived. She considered hitting him over the head with a sofa cushion.

He was uncomfortably sprawled on the living room sofa, one arm trailing on the floor, his face squished into a pillow. With a gulp, Dixie saw that he was wearing a pair of jeans and nothing else.

He looked gorgeous, Dixie thought at once, stumbling to a halt to stare at him. But she pushed that unwelcome idea aside and poked him. "Wake up, sugar. We've got company."

"Mrf?" Flynn mumbled. "Wha—"

"It's morning, see?" Dixie flung open the curtains and a blaze of morning sunlight bounced off Central Park and into the suite with the power of a laser.

Flynn groaned and hid under his pillow.

"Get up, get up," Dixie caroled, deciding to pretend nothing had happened the previous night. "I've got friends coming up in the elevator this minute."

"You're kidding, right?"

"On the contrary," Dixie said, arriving at the suite door in time to open it just as Rob and Jan appeared there.

"Good morning," cried the Munchkins, arm in arm and laughing as usual.

"Not good exactly," Dixie said wryly. For some reason the sight of two happily married people actually enjoying each other's company did not fill her with pleasure this morning.

"Things will improve," Jan promised airily. "We brought coffee and bagels."

"In that case, you may enter," Dixie replied. "And bless you."

The couple barreled into the suite, waving bags of food and lugging two large cardboard cartons. At the theater, the Munchkins were set dressers—employees who made theatrical scenery realistic to the audience by adding details. Their tools were props, fabrics, wallpaper, knickknacks—any items that might make the audience believe the characters onstage were real people. Although young, both Rob and Jan were quickly developing an excellent reputation in the business.

They were a couple of characters themselves, dressing in outlandish clothing that they usually found in vintage-clothing stores. The Munchkins spent all their free time scouring flea markets, tag sales, antique shops and out-of-the-way places nobody else ever heard of in search of wardrobe additions as well as items that could be used effectively in the theater. Professional pack rats, it was clear that they loved their work—and each other.

Rob headed straight for the coffee table to set out a picnic. He stopped dead in his tracks when Flynn sat up from the sofa where he'd been sleeping. "Egad," said Rob. "Is this our hero?"

Flynn glowered at Rob, looking rumpled and grumpy from his night on the sofa. "What's it to you?" he rejoined in a growl.

"Heavens," said Rob as he eyed Flynn with dismay. "You're going to be a challenge, aren't you?"

"Did you bring any newspapers?" Dixie asked.

"No tabloids on Sunday," Jan said. "We'll have to wait until tomorrow for our story to break. That will give us more time to work on Flynn here."

Flynn got up from the sofa with a rumbling grumble and did not answer. He towered over Rob by at least eight inches, and his near-naked state managed to emphasize the animal quality of his body. Without another word, he turned and headed for the bathroom.

Rob blinked and looked at Dixie, clearly stunned by Flynn's physical splendor compared to his own slight stature. "My goodness. Is he for real?"

"Unfortunately, yes," Dixie replied, closing the door of the suite and padding into the room with her friends.

"Unfortunately," Jan observed to her husband, "I think these two got up on the wrong sides of their respective beds this morning."

"Maybe it should have been the same bed," Rob mused.

They laughed merrily, but Dixie found nothing humorous about the situation. "Very funny." She sat down on the sofa and opened one of the deli bags.

Rob and Jan exchanged a look. Then they sat down, too—one on each side of Dixie. They leaned close as she fished a cup of coffee out of the bag for herself.

"Tell us everything, doll," Jan said in a bemused undertone.

"Yes, don't hold back anything, sweetie."

"What are you talking about?"

To her husband, Jan said, "You can cut it with a knife, can't you?"

"A *big* knife," Rob agreed.

"What *are* you talking about?" Dixie demanded, ripping the lid off her coffee cup.

"The sexual tension, dear. Darling, don't you think Dixie looks a little downcast this morning?"

"Poor thing! What do you suppose went wrong?"

"Had a teensy tiff, maybe?"

"With Handsome, you mean? Oh, surely not!"

"Will you two cut it out?"

"O-ho," said Rob. "She's sounding frustrated!"

"*Sexually* frustrated, do you suppose? Not our Dixie! She's immune to that stuff!"

"I am not!" Dixie declared explosively.

"She's not!" Jan crowed. "She's human! Oh, Dixie, do tell us everything! He's a magnificent specimen. We're dying to know the gory details."

"There are no details. There is nothing going on. Flynn has agreed to help us by posing as a big spender from California. At least, I think he's still going to go through with the plan."

"But after last night...?" Rob prodded, but Dixie didn't answer. He popped his eyes at Jan. "My gracious! What do you suppose happened in here?"

Flynn chose that moment to reenter the living room of the suite. He was running one hand through the rumpled hair on his head and managed to look like a tawny cougar emerging from the underbrush. Dixie caught her breath at the sight.

Jan and Rob giggled.

Flynn wasn't feeling fully awake. He'd spent a bad night on the sofa dreaming of cowgirls on motorcycles and chorus lines of gangsters armed with tommy guns and Western omelets. He yawned, then got his first real look at Dixie and forgot about being tired.

She was dressed in a pair of men's pajamas that were decorated with little Wild West cartoons. A pair of bucking broncos leapt over her breasts. Of course, Dixie hadn't fully buttoned up her pajamas, so there was a lot of bare skin showing, too. Her hair was a delightful mess, and her eyes had the sleepy look of a woman who had been kept awake most of the night by dreams of an amorous lover.

*Too bad it wasn't you, buddy,* he grumbled inwardly to himself.

"Good morning," Dixie said coolly. "Did you sleep well?"

"Like a baby," Flynn replied, lying through his teeth.

"Funny," she quipped. "You look terrible."

"You're not exactly looking well rested yourself."

She clenched her teeth, but managed to fake a smile. "These are my friends, Rob and Jan Murdock. They're here to help."

Jan popped up from the sofa. "It's great to meet you, Mr. Flynn. How about some coffee?"

"Just Flynn. Thanks." He accepted a cup from the small woman who appeared to be wearing a yellow tuxedo jacket over a pink T-shirt and a fuchsia miniskirt. Her earrings jangled, and the line of bracelets on her arm sounded like a carnival act.

Jan said, "You're so wonderful to help us this way. If Joey Torrano closes the show, we'll all be in terrible trouble. Why, over two hundred people will be unemployed and—"

Her husband interrupted. "Flynn doesn't need to hear about our problems, Jan. He's being gracious about helping us, so we'll be gracious in return and get right down to business. We want to leave these two alone as soon as possible."

The last thing Flynn wanted just then was to be left alone with Dixie in her adorable pajamas. "Take as much time as you need," he said, opening his cup of coffee. "I need all the help I can get."

Both Jan and Rob looked disappointed.

Thunder appeared on Dixie's brow. "What do you mean by that?"

"Touchy this morning?" Flynn inquired, sipping from his coffee.

"Of course not! I just—I mean— Oo-oh, I think I'll go get dressed."

"Do that," Flynn snapped. "For once, it would be nice to see you fully clothed."

"Why, you— Oh, never mind!" Dixie flounced out of the suite, leaving Jan and Rob looking very curious and amused.

"Well," said Rob when the silence lengthened. "This is fun, isn't it, Jan?"

"Better than anything I've seen in a theater in a long time. Would you like a bagel, Flynn? Then we'll tell you what we have in mind."

Flynn accepted a bagel and attempted to listen while Jan and Rob explained their scheme. They unpacked two cartons of goodies they'd brought from the theater props department and soon began scattering things around the suite—things that looked as if they might belong to a boxer.

"A couple of years ago, we found this shaving kit in a sporting-goods shop in New Jersey," Jan said, holding up a vinyl bag with a razor and soap inside. "Very tacky, but hideously expensive. When we heard you were supposed to be a wealthy boxer, I knew this would be perfect! Shall I leave it in the bathroom in case somebody goes snooping in there?"

"Who would be snooping?"

"Anyone—a spy of Joey's or the police, maybe—"

"Police?"

Rob looked up from unwrapping another prop. "Hasn't Dixie told you? Joey's always being harassed by the police. Surely they've been here dozens of times to rummage around for something to incriminate poor Joey."

"What do you think the police might find?"

"Who knows? Joey's a crook," Jan said, "but we like him. He's been good to the theater, after all."

"By investing dirty money," Flynn responded.

"Money is money," Rob said. "We're desperate. Now, would you like to hear about the rest of the stuff we found for you?"

Flynn pretended to listen to Dixie's friends as they carefully unpacked items and explained their purpose in the elaborate charade.

But his mind was full of Joey Torrano. His job was to do exactly what the theater people didn't want—to find something that might help put Joey behind bars. But so far, Flynn hadn't exactly come up with loads of evidence.

In fact, last night, when he'd been unable to sleep, he'd scouted the suite as thoroughly as possible. He'd managed to turn up assorted bits of Dixie's clothing under furniture and tucked into peculiar places, but he hadn't found much of anything in the way of clues.

A matchbook from a Brooklyn restaurant, that was it.

And how was one stupid matchbook supposed to help?

"We brought you some cigars," Jan continued, presenting Flynn with an unopened box. "We thought these might look authentic for a boxer. They're from this great little smoke shop beside the theater. As a matter of fact, they're the same brand Joey Torrano smokes, I think. Very expensive, illegally smuggled from Cuba through Mexico. We thought they would be a nice touch for your character—a tip-off that you're a little dangerous. What do you think? Do you smoke cigars?"

"Sometimes." Flynn took the box and opened it thoughtfully. The cigars were neatly wrapped. He took one out and studied it while Rob continued to talk.

Then a theory began to form in Flynn's mind. He tried to remember all the facts he'd read in the Torrano file and force them into making some sense with what he'd learned from Dixie Davis.

Maybe there *was* something to be learned from her. He mulled over the idea while Jan and Rob flitted around like a couple of happy chipmunks in a new nest.

When the suite had begun to seem like a new world with all the junk scattered around to look as if a former boxer had moved in, Dixie emerged from her bedroom.

She had put on her wig again, and was dressed to go out in jeans and a big shirt. Was it Flynn's imagination, or had she toned down the sexpot act just a little?

"Ready?" she asked Flynn, pretending to be very businesslike.

"Ready for what?"

"It's Sunday. I have a matinee in a couple of hours. Are you coming?"

"Give me five minutes," Flynn said, heading for the shower.

He had an idea. And he didn't plan on letting Dixie out of his sight. Especially if she went anywhere near the smoke shop where Joey Torrano bought his illegal cigars. There was something going on, Flynn was willing to bet. And by sticking close to Dixie, he was going to find the right clues to put Torrano behind bars.

But when he'd dressed to go out, he discovered Dixie had left without him.

"That little sneak!"

He grabbed his Harley and wheeled it into the hotel elevator.

# Six

***

Dixie had already finished her massage and had begun her warm-up exercises when Flynn finally arrived at the theater.

He was not happy.

"What kept you?" Dixie asked, applying her false eyelashes with care.

"Don't do that again!" He stormed into her dressing room and threw his motorcycle helmet onto her dressing table. Tubes of makeup scattered in all directions.

"Hey!"

"I'm supposed to be looking after you, Miss Davis—"

"You're off the hook," she retorted primly, trying not to notice how gorgeous he looked in one of the outfits chosen from the costume shop. A pale yellow cashmere sweater over khaki trousers made him look handsome and rich. The addition of his leather jacket over it all lent an air of the dangerous renegade. But Dixie was determined to keep her thoughts off Flynn today. "After our discussion last night," she said, "I don't believe I'll need your services anymore."

"The hell you don't," Flynn snapped. "Guess who showed up at the hotel just two minutes after you left?"

Astonished, Dixie dropped her eyelash and spun around on her swivel stool. "Joey? Well, pass me the barbecue! What did you say to him?"

"Nothing. Hotel security managed to keep him contained in the lobby." Flynn began to pace in the small confines of her dressing room. "I slipped out through the kitchen again, which is not easy with a motorcycle, I'll have you know!"

Dixie smothered a giggle at the thought of Flynn skulking out of the Plaza pushing his precious Harley-Davidson.

"He was royally angry that you weren't in the hotel," Flynn said severely. "One of his men punched the concierge."

"Oh, poor Maurice!"

"Yeah, well, I'm the target they're really looking for."

"Oh, sugar, don't worry. Nobody's going to ambush you—not if you stay with the rest of us."

Flynn exploded. "How can I do that when you go running off the minute you have a temper tantrum!"

"I'm sorry," Dixie said, meaning it. She reached out and touched Flynn on the arm. "I didn't mean to leave you in a jam. I won't do it again."

He stared down at her hand, saying nothing.

Hastily, Dixie pulled her hand away. She tried to pretend she hadn't felt the warmth of his skin or the quickening of her own pulse. She picked up her eyelash again and slathered it with glue. "What took you so long to get here? Did your motorcycle conk out along the way?"

"Of course not. I do have a life of my own, you know." Without asking permission, Flynn poured himself a tumbler of water from the glass pitcher Dixie kept on the dressing table. He looked hot and in need of a much stronger drink. "I had some phone calls to make. People to see."

Dixie stuck her eyelash in place. She hadn't really thought about the possibility that Flynn might actually have a life that didn't include her. *See what the theater does to a person? It makes you a complete egomaniac.*

Dixie looked at her reflection in the mirror and sighed. "It's time to go back to Texas."

"What?" Flynn looked down at her, forgetting his drink. "What did you say?"

"Nothing. I was just mumbling. What kind of phone calls? What people?"

"Phone calls," he said, stubbornly refusing to say more. "And people."

She frowned at him in the mirror. "Do you have a girlfriend or something?"

"Would you care?" He met her gaze in the mirror.

Flynn's look challenged Dixie. She felt herself turning very pink and fumbled among her cosmetics for something to keep herself busy. A large brush tumbled into her hand, so she broke the eye contact and dusted powder on her nose. "Of course not. I mean—well, I think of you as a friend—an acquaintance, so naturally I'm interested—curious, er—oh, hell, just answer the question!" She threw down the brush. "Do you have a girl in the wings?"

"The only *girls* in my life," Flynn said, deliberately leaning over her shoulder, "are my sisters Marcie and Nella, who are both still in high school."

Looking at him in the mirror, Dixie became conscious that his chest was making ever so slight contact with her shoulder. She remembered the heat of his gaze as he'd stared at her in the tub last night. The memory made her warm all over again.

"What's that supposed to mean?" she demanded shakily. "Only a real woman is good enough for you?"

He tweaked a lock of her wig. "You said it, I didn't."

"I— You're getting to be damned infuriating, Flynn."

"That makes two of us," he murmured.

The stage manager shouted from the hallway. "Ten minutes, everybody!"

"I'm not warmed up yet!" Dixie yelped, forgetting Flynn's proximity. "And my costume! Flynn, grab my—"

"Forget it," he said, heading for the door. "You can dress yourself this time, Miss Tornado!"

The matinee went smoothly, Dixie thought—for everyone but herself.

She hadn't warmed up sufficiently. Worse yet, she was shaken when she took the stage. She'd allowed Flynn to take her mind off the job she had to do. For the first time since joining the cast of *The Flatfoot and the Floozie,* she'd really felt like an amateur. She'd muffed a line, stumbled during a dance number and nearly missed an entrance.

"What's the matter?" Kiki had asked at the intermission.

"I don't know. Am I really bad?" Dixie had asked anxiously.

"You're not yourself," Kiki had replied diplomatically, putting her arm around Dixie to soothe her. "Just focus on the play, all right? Don't think about Joey."

Joey wasn't the problem.

That was, until after the show.

Dixie rushed down to her dressing room to hide—hoping to avoid the rest of the cast until she could explain herself.

But Flynn was waiting in the hallway several doors down from her own dressing room. In his leather jacket, he melted into the darkness of the hall and surprised the hell out of Dixie when he stepped out and blocked her path.

Dixie tried to brush past him, close to tears. She didn't want to talk to anyone—especially Flynn just then. It was all his fault she'd performed so badly. Her voice trembled. "Why don't you wait out in the hall while I get changed? I just can't face anybody—"

"Then stay out of your dressing room," Flynn snapped, catching her arm and guiding Dixie quickly back the way she'd come. He kept his voice down. "Joey's waiting for you in there."

He propelled Dixie down the hallway, pushing through the rest of the actors as they streamed offstage.

"Joey's here? What does he want? Maybe he's ready to sign a contract!"

Flynn's pace did not slacken. "Jan and Rob talked to him while you were onstage. He didn't bring his lawyer, that's for sure. He wants to slug you."

"Slug me! That'll be the day!" Dixie was steamed. "What's got him so upset?"

"Me, I guess." Flynn seemed to know his way around the theater very well. As they plunged into another hallway and down a flight of stairs that even

Dixie didn't know existed, Flynn explained. "One of the tabloids is running a big story about you and your new love interest in tomorrow's edition. A thoughtful editor figured Joey ought to have an advance copy."

Dixie's spirits rose. "Oh, good! He's furious about you?"

"I suppose that's good from your perspective," Flynn said wryly. "But I like my face the way it is at the moment, and I don't want it rearranged by one of Torrano's goons."

Dixie had to admit she liked Flynn's face, too. But she said, "I can't avoid Joey forever."

"You can avoid him for a couple of days. You won't be able to talk contracts with him yet—not until his jealous rage has cooled off."

That plan made sense to Dixie. "All right, but where are you taking me now? Back to my hotel?"

"Hell, no. If he's got spies in the hotel, he can get one of his leg breakers in there, too."

"Leg breakers!"

Mistaking her exclamation for a question, Flynn said, "Guys who'll get their jollies by breaking your pretty knees if Joey tells them to do it."

"He wouldn't!"

"Oh, wouldn't he?"

To tell the truth, Dixie wasn't sure. She hadn't known Joey Torrano for long, but his reputation was one of a merciless criminal. Of course, she'd only seen his suave side, but Dixie knew she'd only seen Joey under the best of circumstances. Now things were different. If Joey was truly angry at being stood up at their wedding, he might show his true colors.

"Okay," Dixie said, breathless from their run through the tunnels under the theater. "Where in tarnation are we going?"

"My place," Flynn replied, and he dragged Dixie out into the sunlight.

The impact of the sun wasn't nearly as intense as the information he'd just given her. "Your place! Wait, Flynn! I can't—I can't leave in this costume!"

"You're not going back to your dressing room."

"I need some clothes! I can't go out like this!

Flynn spun around and frowned. Then he whipped off his leather jacket and put it around Dixie's shoulders. "There. That'll have to do."

"But I—"

"Leave the wig," he ordered, giving Dixie's fake hair a yank. He tossed the blond wig back into the theater building and then pulled her to the curb. "It'll make you less conspicuous on my bike."

"*On your*—" Dixie resisted when she saw the Harley parked on the street. "Flynn, I can't go riding around the city on your motorcycle while wearing this—this—"

"No choice," he said. "Let's go."

"But—but, Flynn—"

"What's the matter?"

Dixie didn't have the courage to tell him. Truth was, she'd rather sit on a cactus and eat ten pounds of chili peppers than find herself alone with Flynn for any length of time. But she couldn't come up with the words to explain her fear.

"Let's go," he commanded when she stayed silent.

No choice. Dixie climbed onto the back of his motorcycle and held on tight.

Flynn started the bike with a hard kick and revved the noisy engine. The whole machine throbbed with power. The Harley leapt forward and roared down the street. Flynn drove the bike with swift precision, weaving in and out of traffic. The New York streets began to fly by.

Dixie hadn't been in the city long enough to recognize much of anything except 42nd Street and the hotel where she'd been living. She clutched Flynn's chest with both hands, hugging herself tightly against him. She leaned her weight with his as they swung around curves. The motorcycle felt sexy and exciting, she had to admit.

At last Flynn cut down a side street and ended up on a narrow street that seemed packed with cars, trucks, scraggly trees and jump-roping children. A dog leaned out of an open second-floor window and barked at a delivery truck.

On the corner stood a coffee shop that looked busier than any place in Times Square. The revolving door never stopped spinning customers in and out.

Dixie tapped Flynn's chest. "Where are we?"

"A safe neighborhood," he said over his shoulder, gently easing the motorcycle up over the curb and across a couple of yards of cracked sidewalk. The throb of the engine reverberated off brownstone buildings, drawing the attention of a few pedestrians.

Then a gray-haired woman came up a set of steps from a basement apartment. She had a broom in her hand and shaded her flinty eyes from the sun to look at Flynn. She shook her head, pretending annoyance, but when she shouted something to him over the noise of the engine, Dixie heard that her tone sounded more fond than angry.

Flynn waved to her, but kept the motorcycle moving until he'd driven it up the three steps to the front door of a narrow brownstone. Then he cut the engine and bumped open the door with his front wheel.

The woman's voice bellowed up to him. "Patrick Flynn, where do you think you're going with that thing?"

"Hi, Aunt Jane. I'm putting my bike away."

"I thought it was finished! Surely you're going to keep it on the street now that it's not a million pieces all over your apartment!" Although talking about his motorcycle, the woman never took her inquiring gaze from Dixie.

"It's a valuable machine, Aunt Jane. I have to take care of my investment."

"Investment! A motorcycle is a toy, not an investment! And who's this young lady, may I ask? What's she wearing? She's going to catch her death of cold."

"You'll see later, Aunt Jane."

"But . . . but—"

The older woman sputtered, so Dixie gave her a big smile as Flynn rode the bike straight into the building.

Dixie found herself in a dark, cool hallway with a long flight of stairs straight ahead. For an instant she feared Flynn might try to push the motorcycle up to the second floor, but she relaxed when he took a set of keys out of his jeans pocket and unlocked the downstairs door instead.

He put out his hand and helped Dixie off the bike. Then he wheeled the Harley into his apartment ahead of her.

She followed.

The only piece of furniture in the living room was a single sofa.

"Whoa," Dixie said, looking around with interest. "I figured you for a boots-in-the-parlor kind of guy, Flynn. But you haven't got anything at all in your parlor."

"I needed the room to work on my bike," he said, standing the Harley in the center of the room where it appeared to make itself at home.

"I guess this is a New York minimalist apartment, right?"

He grinned. "I've got everything I need."

"Including a nosy relative downstairs."

"The whole neighborhood is full of nosy relatives. Aunt Jane lives downstairs, Uncle Jack upstairs, my cousin Cathy and her kids are across the street. My parents are two blocks down, and Grandad is—"

"Good grief, how many people are in your family?"

"My immediate family? There were seven of us kids. But with all my aunts and uncles, cousins, nieces, nephews, grandparents—well, we had sixty-two at Thanksgiving last year."

Dixie blew an astonished whistle and closed the door behind herself. "I guess you like big families."

Amused, he said, "I go broke every Christmas."

Dixie strolled farther into the apartment, her tap shoes ringing on the polished oak floor. She wanted to get to know the place and how it felt to be there. She could learn a lot about the man by studying his home. So far, it felt a lot like the Flynn she knew—careful and cautious.

She sauntered around and peeked into the kitchen. "So how come you're not married, Patrick Flynn? How come there aren't a bunch of little Patricks running around?"

He shrugged. "I've been busy, I guess. Let's find you something to wear, okay?"

"I'd be grateful."

Dixie tagged along as Flynn left the sitting room, cut through a narrow kitchen, past a neat bathroom and into the apartment's single bedroom, which was barely big enough for the bed and a gigantic antique armoire. The bed had been made in a haphazard fashion—the comforter thrown over the rest of the bedclothes. Dixie was glad to see that the rest of the room was a little messy, too. He'd left some clothes in a pile on the floor, a pair of sneakers lay half under the bed. A newspaper had been forgotten on the bedside table and a fishing rod leaned against the armoire.

A closet door leaned partway open, revealing a clutter of belongings—a scuba tank, some clothing, a shelf of books. The walls were decorated with some framed photographs of people—presumably members of the large Flynn clan—a Matisse print and a poster advertising the island of Anguilla.

"A motorcycle mechanic who goes scuba diving in the Caribbean," Dixie mused.

"I like to get out of the city when I have time off." Flynn opened the armoire. It housed a small television on the top shelf and assorted clothes in the drawers below. He began rooting around for something Dixie could wear.

"I thought all New Yorkers loved their city."

"Some do. At the moment, I'm not exactly enchanted."

Dixie leaned against the armoire to get a better look at Flynn's face. "Oh, yeah? How come?"

"Let's just say I'm starting to think about moving to the suburbs."

"Away from your family?"

"No, I'd like them to come along. My brother, you see . . ."

Flynn seemed to catch himself. He pretended to decide between two identical blue shirts and finally passed one to Dixie. "Here, this ought to be all right."

"Your brother?" Dixie prompted, wanting to hear more. Suddenly she knew there was something worth listening to. For once, Flynn had let his caution slip.

"Nothing." Flynn straightened and attempted to erase his thoughts from his face. "I don't think my jeans will fit you. Any ideas?"

"You have any boxers?"

"I'm a jockey shorts kind of guy, to tell the truth. How about some running shorts?"

"Fine. And a belt?"

"In here." He opened the closet and rummaged around on the shelves for a moment.

"What about your brother?" Dixie asked again.

A pause. Then, "I shouldn't have mentioned it."

"Him," Dixie corrected. "I want to know. What's his name?"

"Sean."

"Sean and Patrick Flynn." Dixie liked the sound of that. "Does he live in the neighborhood?"

"He used to." Flynn was busy with the clothing. "He helped me rebuild the Harley. He was really into bikes. But he was in the wrong place at the wrong time last fall."

A rush of dread filled Dixie. "Oh, Flynn—"

"He's not dead." Flynn was suddenly very still. "He was shot, though, during a holdup at a take-out shop a few blocks from here. It was pretty bad, but Sean should be able to walk eventually. He's spending some time in a rehab hospital. When he gets out—well, I hope he'll move out of the city."

"New York is full of crime," Dixie said on a sigh.

"And criminals," Flynn agreed, his voice hardening. "Like Joey Torrano."

He passed a pair of white shorts to Dixie, and fixed her with a steady gaze. "Torrano's a bad character, Dixie. You should stay away from him."

She put her defenses up immediately. "I don't mind him. Maybe I don't exactly want to marry him, but I—"

"He's a crook, an abuser, a thief. And probably a murderer, too."

"There's no proof of that," Dixie began weakly.

Flynn took her arms in his hands and squeezed. "Damn it, do you really know what you're doing? Conning a jerk into financing your show—isn't there some other way?"

"We need his money," Dixie said just as fiercely. "What better way to use it than keeping a few hundred honest souls at work? Supporting the arts, making people happy—"

"But he ought to be in jail!"

"I intend to get his money first," Dixie snapped.

"Dixie—"

"Let me change my clothes," she said quickly. "I feel naked all of a sudden."

Flynn turned away sharply. "So what else is new?" he muttered.

Dixie's temper began to flare. Throttling the anger back, she said, "Listen, Flynn, you can take me back to my hotel right now if—"

"No, that's out of the question."

The finality in his voice enraged her. "Am I a *prisoner* here?"

"Don't tempt me!"

"I'm not crazy about staying in your place, you know. Why, you live like a monk and—"

"I'm not thinking like a monk," he replied, eyeing her costume with a glitter in his eyes. "And if you think having a half-dressed showgirl in my apartment is easy, you'd better think again!"

Dixie glared at him. But the thought of spending the night in his apartment—his one-bedroom apartment—suddenly dawned on her. In an instant she found herself trembling. *Don't be an idiot,* she thought to herself. *He's a perfect gentleman. He's careful about everything he does and says. He's not impulsive like you, so relax.*

Dixie wasn't so sure she was capable of behaving herself with the same decorum Flynn had displayed.

She spun around and headed for the bathroom. "I'll get changed now."

"Good. Are you hungry?"

"Starved."

"I'll go see what I can pick up across the street." He followed her down the hall a few steps, then turned back. "Uh, don't answer the phone if it rings. I mean, there's no need to. The answering machine will get my calls."

"What's the matter? Afraid I'm going to shock your family?"

Flynn gave her a steely look and didn't answer. Dixie closed the bathroom door. A few minutes later she heard Flynn leave his apartment.

Flynn escaped his place and fled across the street to the neighborhood coffee shop. He slid onto a stool at the counter and nodded at Roy, the owner of the place, who waved. On his next trip behind the counter, Roy tossed Flynn a paper menu of the day's specials. Flynn pretended to study the Sunday choices, although he knew them by heart.

But his mind was full of Dixie. In his apartment she'd looked even more delectable than ever—more real, somehow. And Flynn ached to touch her, hold her, kiss her.

*What in hell possessed you to bring her here?* he asked himself. *You're never going to make it through the night unless you stand under the cold shower for eight hours straight.*

Someone slipped onto the stool next to him, interrupting his thoughts. Flynn turned.

His aunt Jane smiled over the rims of her librarian-style half glasses. "Well, darling, care to tell your old aunt what's going on?"

"Sorry, Aunt Jane. Police business."

"Don't give me that line, Patrick. The young lady I saw didn't look like a gangster. That's what you're supposed to be working on now, right? Gangsters and organized crime?"

Flynn couldn't help smiling. "You know I can't talk about my work, Aunt Jane. What if a mobster decides to kidnap you, tie you to a chair and make you tell everything you know?''

''I'd die first,'' she said with a grin, patting his hand. ''But I'll let you off the hook this time. She's very pretty.''

''Who?''

''The young lady I didn't notice going into your apartment.''

Flynn suppressed a smile. He loved Aunt Jane. She was his mother's sister and the family eccentric. Jane painted pet portraits and made a very good living for herself—and her four cats. She also devoted large amounts of time to the local animal shelter, and she was known as the lady to take your puppy to if the vet's office was closed and you needed help right away.

''All right,'' Flynn said. ''Let's change the subject before I have to arrest you for interfering with police business. What's new?''

''What's new is that my nephew is finally getting his life back.''

''Aunt Jane—''

''Believe me, I'm delighted, Patrick. You should have a love interest again.''

''She's not my love interest.''

''Maybe she should be.''

''It's not like I've been completely out of circulation.''

''You call one dinner with your second cousin a date?''

''You've been keeping track! I can't believe it!'

Jane did not get flustered by the accusation. "A real girlfriend, that's what you need. You shouldn't be thinking about Sean all the time."

"I'm not thinking about Sean."

"Don't get grumpy."

"I'm *not* grumpy!"

Aunt Jane waved at the diner's owner, beckoning him over. "Roy, Patrick has a young lady at his place for dinner tonight. What do you have in the way of a romantic menu?"

With a grin, Roy exclaimed, "That's good news! I got just what he needs. Coming right up."

"Wonderful. It'll be my treat."

Flynn knew it was useless to try stopping Roy, who had been enamored of Jane since forever and was still willing to go the extra mile to gain her affections. "Aunt Jane, I'm not a kid anymore. You don't have to treat me like a—"

"I want to spoil you." She reached over and straightened his collar. "You deserve some spoiling. You've been miserable far too long."

"I have not!"

"Don't deny it. We've watched you mourn for months. And there's nothing to be mourning about, Patrick. Nobody died. Everything's fine."

"Everything?"

"Sean's getting better. You can't ask for more."

"I wish it hadn't happened."

"You can't change the past."

"I could have done something."

"Like what?" Jane asked with a disbelieving laugh.

"I'm a cop. I'm supposed to prevent crime."

"Oh, Patrick. Not everywhere." She leaned closer. "Darling, you can't be the guardian angel of everyone in the city."

"I ought to be able to protect my own family."

"Sean's a big boy. He shouldn't have been out at that time of night and he knows it. Don't carry this guilt around forever, darling."

It was an old argument. Flynn tried to wave it off. "Okay, okay. I'll work on it."

"I think you've made a good start with your young lady."

"She's *not* my young lady." After a thought, Flynn added, "Not exactly."

"Well, do something about that!" Jane ordered, laughing. "She's very pretty. Is she nice?"

"Nice, yes. A bit of a character."

"Wonderful! You need some spice in your life."

"She's plenty spicy." Flynn laughed.

"Is she a good girl, though? Not one of those—well, someone you might catch something from?"

"No, Aunt Jane," Flynn assured her, certain of the truth. "She's a good girl."

"Well, then, what's keeping you? Roy, is that food ready yet?"

Roy had already approached, carrying two large paper bags he had packed with food and drink. Some bottles clinked in one bag, and the fragrance of warm food tickled Flynn's nose.

"All ready," said Roy. "Guaranteed to melt the heart of any woman in the world."

"Perfect!" cried Aunt Jane. "Now go for it, Patrick!"

# Seven

*What the hell,* he thought, crossing the street. *We're both consenting adults. What have I got to lose?*

He was hardly aware that rain had started to pelt down in a summer storm until he'd reached the stoop of his building and realized water was dripping off his hair.

Shaking like a spaniel, he slammed back into his apartment. He stopped in the doorway, arms full of paper bags, to see Dixie curled up on his sofa, wearing his clothes and apparently darning his socks. Funny how sexy a woman could look wearing a man's clothes.

She looked up and grinned with the familiar Texan sparkle in her eyes—a hint that there was plenty of spark inside her, too. "You're supposed to say, 'Honey, I'm home!' "

Flynn kicked the door shut behind himself, absurdly glad to see that she hadn't run off. He'd half expected her to steal his Harley and escape. He asked, "What are you doing?"

She held up a needle and the thread she was about to pass through the eye. "Darning a sock. See?"

"That's my sock! Where did you get it?"

"It was on the bathroom floor. Look at the holes! I thought I'd fix it. I'm pretty good at darning socks." She bit her lower lip and concentrated on threading the needle. "Granny Butterfield taught me this the same summer I learned her fan dance routine, I think."

She was perched on the sofa with her feet tucked up under her, leaning toward the rain-washed window for light. There was a faint halo around her short hair, but Dixie looked anything but angelic. She had tied the loose ends of his shirt up around her midriff and tightly cinched his shorts around her narrow waist. Her face was washed clean of makeup, making Dixie look ten years younger than before—though hardly innocent.

She looked so domestic that Flynn didn't have the heart to tell her the sock she'd chosen to mend was the one he kept around for his sister's mutt, Noodles, to chew on when he visited.

Flynn's chest expanded in a weird way at the sight of Dixie diligently trying to mend his sock.

Still balancing the bags from Roy, Flynn crossed the floor and leaned down over Dixie, dripping rainwater. She looked up, startled.

He murmured, "Honey, I'm home."

Instinctively, he kissed her. Dixie's eyes were wide, but she dropped her mending and met his kiss with her mouth primly raised. He liked the taste of her, the texture of her lips and the suggestion of sensuality that lingered on her tongue as he parted her mouth. Then he broke the contact, thinking he'd rushed things.

But oddly enough, Dixie reached up with both hands to touch his wet face. For a second, Flynn wasn't sure what to expect. Then she pulled him down once more, closed her eyes and kissed him back, long and slow.

Flynn's insides turned hot and syrupy. His brain immediately began to indulge in erotic fantasies. Somehow he managed to drop the paper bags on the sofa and run his fingers deeply into her wispy soft hair to hold the kiss a little longer. She was deliciously sweet and eager. Clearly, she had no idea how much pent-up desire he felt for her or she wouldn't have risked a second kiss. Flynn had a hell of a time holding on to his self-control.

Dixie broke the kiss gently.

"You have a lot of nerve," she said, a smile in her gaze and her hand still on his cheek.

"For what?"

"Holding me prisoner and now torturing me like this."

"Funny, but I don't call kissing torture."

"I meant the food. It smells terrific."

Flynn fought back his frustration with a comic groan. "You're starving, right?"

"When do we eat?"

"Right now, if you like." But Flynn spent a split second wishing she would prefer to do something else first.

"Where's your table?" she asked, disappointing the hell out of him.

"Haven't got one."

"Really? Where do you eat?"

"Out, mostly. Or," he added truthfully, "in bed."

The idea didn't horrify her. In fact, Dixie's smile widened. "What are you trying to do, sugar? Seduce me?"

"Let's eat," he suggested, avoiding the question.

Dixie figured she was playing with fire, but she led the way to Flynn's bedroom and helped unpack the food. Soon the heady scents of wet pastrami sandwiches and kosher pickles filled the air.

"I should have known this would be Roy's idea of a romantic dinner," Flynn muttered, shaking his head over the feast.

"Who's Roy?" Dixie asked, climbing onto the bed and settling down Indian-style to enjoy the meal.

"A guy in the neighborhood. One who's got a crush on Aunt Jane." Flynn stripped off his wet shirt and took a worn pullover from the armoire. While Dixie's breath caught in her throat as she glimpsed his broad chest and rugged shoulders, he pulled the dry sweater over his head and approached the bed.

Dixie moved over to make room for him. "I never figured city people had neighborhoods like we do in Texas." Dixie unwrapped a sandwich and inhaled its fragrance. Her stomach growled hungrily.

"Of course we do. We just don't have picket fences and miles of lawn between our homes."

"My family doesn't have a picket fence. Or any lawn, for that matter. It's too dry. Daddy's ranch is practically in the desert."

"He's got a ranch?" Flynn asked, climbing onto the bed, too. He plucked a pickle from one of the wrapped packages and chomped it in two. "You mean, a cattle ranch? Real Texas stuff?"

"Llamas," Dixie told him around a mouthful of pastrami. "Mmm. This is great! I love messy sandwiches."

"Then you're a woman of simple, but refined taste." Flynn chose a sandwich for himself and unwrapped it. "Tell me about llamas in Texas."

So Dixie told him. Licking her fingers, she started with how her father's crackpot scheme to turn llamas into a cash crop had failed miserably, but the peculiar animals had turned out to be a big hit with exotic pet lovers. Then she found herself telling Flynn about her assorted relatives—not just Granny Butterfield, but her cousin Jake, who was a Texas Ranger, Uncle Floyd the Baptist minister who also bottled Creole hot sauce in Louisiana, and the infamous Sweet Creek recluse,

Spike Denison, who had lived just down the road all their lives but had never been seen by any member of the Davis clan.

"How do you know he exists if you've never seen him?" Flynn asked.

"You don't have to lay eyes on a man to know he's around," Dixie replied, sampling the pickles. "He drinks two cases of beer every nine days, and his mama orders seven extra-large pepperoni pizzas—one every night of the week. You can't tell me a little bitty woman like her drinks all that beer and eats pizza for her midnight snacks!"

"Maybe she has a dog that likes Italian food."

Dixie shook her head, leaning closer to confide the rest of the story. "It's Spike, all right. Doc Martinez says he delivered the baby forty years ago, but nobody's ever seen old Miz Denison digging a grave or canning a lot of extra rattlesnake meat, so he's got to exist."

Flynn cracked up laughing. "You're making this up!"

"Am not!" Dixie cried. "Cross my heart, every word is true!"

Flynn listened to her stories, bemused and entertained. He relaxed on the bed, kicking off his boots and plumping the pillows for both of them to lean against. It felt like a Roman banquet to Dixie—lying there among his comfortable bedclothes and wolfing down the New York fare. Bottles of flavored seltzer waters washed down the thick sandwiches.

Outside, rain pelted against the windows and an occasional flash of lightning made Dixie look up from her food. But most of the time, she found herself mesmerized by Flynn's face. He listened and watched, laughing and sometimes questioning her further. He paid close attention to her tales, but Dixie sometimes wondered if his mind was totally on the subject at hand.

She caught him glancing at her bare legs once in a while, and he seemed to find excuses to lean close to her—like choosing another pickle or opening a second bottle to quench his thirst.

It was cozy and fun, Dixie decided as the evening gathered outside. During her stay in New York, she hadn't had time to get close to anyone. And here was Flynn—attractive and protective and—well, *he's the best thing to blow into your life in a long time, honey.*

He had a sexy mouth, she decided. And an observant gaze. When she found herself admiring the breadth of his shoulders, he knew what she was looking at. Dixie blushed, and his response was a quick smile that he tried to hide.

There was something else on his mind, however. She knew he wasn't just thinking about sex, but she was afraid to ask. The light in his eyes was full of humor, yet thoughtful and speculative, too. Flynn was unlike the men she'd been with before. Compared to him, they suddenly seemed like boys. Although Flynn had a playful side, there was a darker corner of his soul that Dixie hadn't quite figured out.

"Dessert?" he suggested when the sandwiches were demolished. The bed looked as if the entire Confederate army had marched through.

"I couldn't!" Dixie sighed, and lay down among the pillows. She stretched, satisfied. "I'm stuffed—unless there's chocolate, of course."

Flynn tore his gaze from the length of her body and peeked into the last remaining container. "It's chocolate," he confirmed. "Cannoli."

Dixie groaned. "I can't possibly—"

But when Flynn drew one of the luscious pastries out, she weakened. "Oh, maybe just a bite."

He leaned down on one elbow and held out the cannoli. Dixie tried to take a judicious nibble, but she ended up laughing and dribbling whipped cream down her chin.

The most natural reaction in the world was to tilt her chin upward so Flynn could lick off the cream.

He did. Slowly. And watching her eyes with his during every sensuous moment. His tongue was rough as a cat's and just as careful.

Meeting his warm gaze, Dixie didn't have to swallow the bite in her mouth. Instead it melted down her throat with silky smoothness.

Next thing she knew, Flynn was kissing her deeply. The pastry, forgotten, slipped from his hands as he ran his fingers into her hair and toppled Dixie back into the pillows. His chest collided with hers—solid and warm. The rest of his body was suddenly aligned with hers. His knee rode gently between her two softer ones. The bedclothes made a soft squishy sound as they gave beneath the weight of two bodies easing down among them. Flynn tasted hot and delicious. Dixie's head swam.

*This is crazy,* cried a far-off voice inside her head. *You've only known him a few days—barely long enough to decide if you like him!*

Oh, but she liked him. A lot. Not just the way he kissed or touched her or the way he listened and protected her. There was a kinship underneath all the banter. A connection Dixie couldn't describe.

But she responded to it. Tentatively, Dixie slid her arms around his neck. She played her fingertips in the swirl of hair at the back of his head. Growing bolder, she parted her lips and tasted his tongue as it swiped hers with agonizing sweetness. She released a sigh of longing.

Flynn kissed her mouth a long while, then traced his lips along her cheek, her temples. He blew a breath along her hairline. Dixie began to tremble and held on tighter.

"Flynn, this is—it feels so good, but it's against all my rules."

"Some rules ought to be broken."

"But I'm— I've got to be careful. So many men— In this city, everybody wants me. I'm the flavor of the week in the tabloids—"

"You're the most delicious flavor I've ever tasted." He nibbled her earlobe, sending electric shivers down her nerve endings.

"But—"

"You want me, too. I can feel it."

He must have felt her hard nipples straining through her clothing. Or maybe he heard the thunder of blood rushing in her veins. "I do," she said, voice shaking. "But this is too fast for me."

"I thought," he murmured, pressing more soft kisses down the column of her throat, "this was nice and slow."

Dixie quivered all over, knowing she should resist, but finding herself totally weakened by his love-making. It was very slow, all right. Slow like a long fuse. Dixie could feel a huge explosion building up inside herself.

"Flynn—"

"Okay," he breathed, halting the deliberate strand of kisses he'd been bestowing on her goose-bumped skin. Propping himself on his elbows, he said, "Okay, we'll stop."

"Good."

"As long as you're sure—"

"I'm sure." Dixie sighed.

"Uh, Dixie?"

"Mmm?"

"You have to let me go."

Dixie smiled, but kept her arms locked around his neck to prevent Flynn from abandoning her just yet. "I know," she murmured. "I will. Let's talk first."

"First?"

"Tell me your biggest secret."

"My—" For once, he seemed truly puzzled.

"There's something you're keeping from me. I can feel it."

He shook his head. "Dixie, I—"

"Have you got a deep, dark secret, Patrick Flynn?"

He was quiet so long that Dixie opened her eyes and looked into his face. But Flynn looked far away at that moment. As if wrestling with a thought.

Still soft, Dixie said, "I want to know you, Patrick. Not about your family or your neighborhood or your motorcycle. But you."

He gave her a ghost of a grin. "My motorcycle is important to me."

"So I've noticed," she said wryly. "But I mean—"

"I know, I know. But the Harley is—well, it's a lot of things to me. My brother helped me pick it out in the first place. And he helped me rebuild it. It's taken me forever, but now..."

Dixie didn't speak. She waited.

And Flynn began to tell her haltingly about his brother Sean.

About Sean as a boy, Flynn's little brother who tagged along with the big boys. About Sean who got mediocre grades in school, but loved football and cars. And motorcycles. About how he'd started hanging out with bikers and joined a gang—not a bunch of whiskey-drinking hell-raisers, but a group of guys who rode together and worked on their machines by the hour.

Then about how Sean had ended up in a store during a late-night holdup. It was an accident. One of those random tragedies that rendered an innocent bystander into a cripple.

"His shooting," Flynn said finally, "was the worst thing that's ever happened to me. I felt so helpless, so responsible, so—oh, damn, I don't know. It's been my whole life for almost a year. But now, suddenly you're here and—I can't explain it. Now things are changing. I feel like I'm coming out of a tunnel."

Dixie stroked the dark hair at Flynn's temples, trying desperately to memorize the expression on his face, in his eyes. This was it—the look she'd first seen when she'd run out of the church and found exactly what she'd been looking for—a man with a heart. A man with feelings that ran deep.

"You can't feel guilty forever," Dixie murmured.

Again the unhappy smile crossed his mouth. "That's what Aunt Jane says."

"Aunt Jane is a smart lady."

Flynn's eyes lightened. "She told me to come over here tonight and seduce the hell out of you. She even bought us dinner."

Dixie smiled. "Did she, now?"

"She thinks you're pretty."

"What do you think?"

"I think you're beautiful," Flynn whispered. "Without your wig and all that makeup and the Wild West outfits. I've never seen a more beautiful woman than the one who's with me right now, Diana."

He eased down again, taking Dixie's very willing mouth with his once more. They coupled with greater understanding than before, and greater passion. Dixie felt a lavalike heat overflow inside herself as she arched to fit her body against his harder frame.

She longed for the kissing to go on forever.

But gradually Dixie became aware of a telephone. The persistent ring finally penetrated her brain. Flynn stiffened an instant later.

"Phone," Dixie whispered.

"I better get it."

"If it's Aunt Jane, say thanks for the dinner. I loved every bite."

Reluctantly, Flynn eased himself off Dixie and reached across the bed for the insistent telephone. He picked up and dragged the receiver down onto the pillow with him. He said only, "Flynn."

A male voice at the other end began to talk. Flynn listened without moving, but Dixie sensed at once that his mind had suddenly left her.

She crept out of the bed and gathered the remains of their picnic. Carrying the mess to the kitchen, she cleaned up and then let herself into Flynn's bathroom. She could hear him answering questions with monosyllabic responses.

Closing the door and turning on the light, Dixie looked at herself in the mirror. She looked the same, but she felt monumentally different.

*Adults don't always play by rules,* Dixie told herself.

Dixie always had. It was safe to keep her behavior within a certain framework. Granny Butterfield had known that long ago when she'd been in the Ziegfeld Follies. A woman who didn't know her limits then was doomed to get herself into big trouble.

But those days were gone, Dixie thought. Women could be more than beauty queens with no assets but their faces and pretty legs. So maybe it was time Dixie grew with the times, too.

She'd always known who she was. Always known what she wanted out of life.

Now, she wanted Flynn. Even if it ended up being for one night, she wanted him.

And basically, she was an impulsive person. She liked to act instead of do a lot of thinking. Better to make a mistake than do nothing, had been her motto—except when it came to matters of the heart.

Maybe it was time to be impulsive there, too.

She certainly hadn't had much luck in love before.

In the bedroom, Flynn heard the bathroom door close quietly, and he finally let himself pay full attention to his caller.

"Sergeant," he said, keeping his voice down, "she's here right now. I had to get her out of the theater today because Torrano was raving like a lunatic. I was afraid he might harm her."

"She's at *your* place?" Kello demanded, disbelieving. "Now? This minute?"

"She's out of the room at the moment, but—"

"Flynn, are you insane? This is a mobster's girlfriend we're talking about! What you're doing is completely against police procedure!"

"I had to do something. I didn't want her to get hurt—or worse. Torrano was insane with jealousy."

"Jealousy? Exactly what are you doing with his girlfriend, Flynn?"

"Looking after her safety. I brought her here because Torrano doesn't know me from Adam. She'll be all right here—at least, safer than she is dancing on a Broadway stage. You have a better idea?"

"No, no, I suppose not. You had to improvise." Kello blew an irritated sigh. "Okay, what have you learned so far? Anything we can use?"

"There's a restaurant in Brooklyn I think we ought to look into."

"Oh, yeah?"

Flynn gave his sergeant the name and address he'd found on the matchbook left in Dixie's apartment. "It may be nothing," Flynn said, "but I seem to remember reading the name of this restaurant in a report a while back. Maybe there's something to be learned there."

"You could be right. I think I remember the name, too. I'll ask the rest of the guys what they know. Okay, what else?"

"There's a smoke shop near the theater where Dixie's show is playing."

"Dixie?" repeated Kello. "I thought she was Miss Davis during the first half of this conversation?"

"Whatever. About the smoke shop."

"Yeah?"

"It was closed today before the matinee, so I didn't go inside. But I thought we'd better check it out—see who owns the place, what goes on in there. Maybe there's something."

"What do you think is going on?"

"The Mexico connection. I think we ought to explore it. If we can't get Torrano for all the other stuff he's done, maybe we ought to nail him for the illegal aliens he's got working all over the city."

Sergeant Kello mulled that over for a while and finally murmured, "The way Eliot Ness and his boys got Capone for tax evasion?"

"Either way, he goes to jail. That's what we want, right?"

"Right." Kello considered the idea for several more moments. "Okay, what's your plan?"

"We need some help from Immigration."

"I know a lady over there. She's good, too."

"Ask her to share what they've got on Torrano. Maybe we can put our heads together and come up with enough evidence."

"In the meantime, you're putting pressure on the Davis woman?"

The bathroom door opened, and Flynn looked up in time to see Dixie slip into the bedroom. His mouth went dry and he couldn't respond to the sergeant.

She was naked.

And if the sight of America's favorite showgirl completely dressed was enough to make men crazy, Dixie naked was a sight to paralyze the strongest man on earth.

"Flynn?" asked Sergeant Kello. "The Davis woman. Are you learning anything about Torrano from her?"

Flynn opened his mouth to speak, but no sound came out.

"Flynn," said Kello testily, "are you there?"

Dixie turned off the light and advanced toward the bed—bold as brass in the half-light. Her skin was creamy white all over. Her legs were endlessly long. Her breasts were perfectly symmetrical, gracefully blending into a slim waist and flaring gently into the curve of her hips. Her smile glimmered. Frozen on the bed, Flynn couldn't have answered the sergeant if his life depended on it.

"Flynn? Flynn?"

At last, Flynn made his voice work. "Gotta go," he rasped, and then he dazedly handed the receiver into Dixie's waiting hand.

She took the receiver and cradled it gently, hanging up on Sergeant Kello without taking her smoldering gaze from Flynn's. When the phone was hung up, she said, "I couldn't wait any longer."

She climbed onto the bed and straddled Flynn's motionless frame, pinning his hips to the bedclothes by gently clasping them with her exquisitely shaped thighs. She put her hands on his chest. "You don't mind, do you?"

Flynn slid his hands along the slender length of her arms. "Mind?"

"I want to make love," Dixie whispered. "All night."

"Dixie—"

"I've thought about it. I don't do this kind of thing, you know. I've never slept with any man I wasn't married to." Slowly, she slid Flynn's pullover over his belly and ran her hands under it to caress his chest. "Didn't I tell you?"

"Yes, but—" He tried to concentrate on what she was saying, but Dixie's feather-soft touch was causing short circuits in his nervous system. The reality of such a beautiful woman in his bed was almost more than he could handle.

"My first marriage was a high school thing." Dixie ran her fingernails along the ridge of Flynn's collarbone. "I did love him, and he loved me. But it wasn't forever. We were kids."

"And . . . and the second?"

"An older man," Dixie said with a smile. "He was thirty, and I was twenty-five. I know now he was looking for a trophy wife. We only lasted a few months. Since then—for two years now—I've kept my heart under lock and key."

"It's been two years?"

"Since I've been with a man, yes. So, Flynn—"

"If you ask me to be gentle, I think you'd better know right now it may be impossible."

She laughed, and her thighs tightened around his hips. "No, that's not it. I just—I want you to warn me now if you think I'll regret this."

"I thought Dixie Davis never regrets anything."

"True," she murmured thoughtfully.

"I can't make promises," he said after a moment. "Not unless I'm sure I can keep them. But I want to protect you, Diana. I want you to be safe."

"I think I am with you."

"Is that enough?"

"Maybe," she whispered, sliding down to kiss him with her smiling mouth. "I hope so."

It was a soft kiss, nothing more than a graze, really. But instantly her lips rekindled the desire Flynn had managed to fight back since the phone had rung. He flattened both hands on her shoulders and smoothed down the curves of her back. Her bottom felt smooth as marble, but as warm as if she'd just walked off the beach.

Her naked breasts pressed against his bare chest caused the most erotic results. Suddenly his whole body was on fire. Then her tongue slipped into his mouth and worked a fiery magic, too. His blood seemed to boil. Flynn moaned deep in his throat, and pulled Dixie more tightly against himself. Surely she felt how hard he was. She seemed to weaken with unspoken desire.

*Don't break her heart,* warned his conscience. *Don't hurt this woman, Flynn. If you make love now and walk out of her life tomorrow, she'll never forgive you.*

Worse, he thought dimly, you'll never forgive yourself.

But he couldn't stop. She was too perfect, too sensual. The slender lines and full curves of her body combined with a certain sweet vulnerability in her soul—a combination Flynn couldn't resist.

"I want to touch you everywhere," he murmured when her lips slid from his and traveled slowly down his neck and chest. He writhed beneath her, clutching Dixie hard when she licked his flat, male nipples.

"Then do," Dixie whispered back.

He rolled and pressed Dixie down into the bed. In a single yank, he pulled his pullover over his own head and then dived down to lie against her bare body. He let his hand roam over her breasts, along her ribs, across her belly. He swiped a caress across the tops of her thighs and watched Dixie shudder with excitement. She was quick to respond. Her breath caught in her throat, and her eyes were luminous.

It was like a dream to Dixie. Flynn was slow and gentle, despite the hammering of his heart. He was intensely aroused and fought hard to hold back. She let him have his way with her, and she'd never experienced anything so wonderfully exciting. He was breathless, panting, covering her with his mouth and tongue, whispering how beautiful she was.

He tasted her everywhere. Dixie's head spun with the delights he aroused in her.

She tugged off the rest of his clothes, anxious to take their passion to the next level.

"I can't wait, Flynn."

"I want to go on all night."

He had enough wits left to remember to open a drawer beside the bed. He groped for a foil packet, and Dixie laughed when he dropped the first one, cursing.

"How like you to be careful!" she teased.

"You're the one who's been abstinent."

"I was just waiting for the right moment to be my usual impulsive self."

"I'm glad you waited."

She had waited, she thought with a smile. For the right man, not just the right time. And here he was— sweet and kind and sexy as hell.

She helped him with the condom, caressing until Flynn bit back an erotic growl.

With a supple roll, he had her down on the bed again. Rougher this time, he kissed Dixie all over and followed each kiss with a caress that left her gasping.

Then she drew him inside. Because it had been so long for her, she gave a gasp at first, but then it felt wonderfully good. He was deep inside her after that, moving with the gentle persistence of a tide.

Dixie cried out as the waves crashed over her. She let the swirling darkness consume her, drowning her voice, releasing every nerve in a swift implosion of pleasure.

Flynn came after Dixie, unleashing his passion in a powerful rush after holding back for her sake.

They sank down in the bedclothes after that, sated and deliciously exhausted. They talked nonsense for a while—hungry words. Then Flynn's caresses began again—slowly at first. Dixie found herself exploring his body, too. He was beautiful in his own way. So strong.

So insatiable.

Before sleep overcame her hours later, Dixie remembered worrying for a few seconds. *Maybe this was a mistake.* But Flynn gathered her close and put his nose against her throat, to sleep. He murmured her name very softly. Her real name.

With a smile, Dixie drifted off to sleep, too.

# Eight

On Monday morning Dixie woke up and said, "There's no performance on Mondays. We can stay in bed all day."

On Tuesday morning, Dixie said, "What I love most about New York is restaurants that deliver. Do you know how long it's been since I've put on any clothes?"

"I know," Flynn said with a gleam in his eye as he tugged the bedclothes down to reveal her naked limbs. "Believe me, I know."

For lunch they ate fried rice from the Chinese restaurant around the corner. The food was delivered by a teenage boy who never blinked at the sheet Flynn wore wrapped around his hips to answer the door for the third time in two days.

Afterward, Flynn teased Dixie's breasts with a chopstick until she giggled helplessly. She had fun with Flynn. Although there had been moments of profound emotion, she found his laughter her greatest pleasure. It was good to see him let go and enjoy himself.

Aunt Jane called after lunch and Flynn answered reluctantly. He felt as if he'd landed in paradise, and he hated to break the spell.

"Patrick," Aunt Jane asked, "do you still have that pretty young lady staying with you?"

"You know I do, Aunt Jane." Flynn lay back on the pillows and dragged the receiver with him. "You watch my door like a hawk."

"All right, all right," she conceded. "Well, I just thought I'd tell you that your whole family has recognized your picture in the paper."

"What picture?"

"*All* the pictures," Aunt Jane said severely. "Even with that silly mustache, your brothers and sisters knew you at once. But they're all too polite to telephone you to find out which parts of the story are true."

Flynn surrendered the chopstick to Dixie. "What story, Aunt Jane?"

"The tabloids are saying you're a boxer, darling, and they say you're keeping company with that dancer from *The Flatfoot and the Floozie*. Well, we *know* you're not a boxer—unless you count those years in school with Father O'Brien—so what's going on?"

Flynn had hoped the rest of the world might disappear so he could have Dixie in his bed forever. But reality had returned, and he sighed. "Can I tell you in a couple of days?"

"Is it police stuff?"

"Yes," said Flynn, conscious that Dixie was very close but apparently not listening. She feathered the chopstick through the hair on Flynn's chest and kept moving lower, clearly with no idea she was playing with fire.

"Goodness—how cloak-and-dagger! Just one more thing," said Aunt Jane. "That young lady of yours—is she from Texas, by any chance?"

"Yes," said Flynn, intercepting the chopstick by grasping Dixie's hand. Already, he was rock hard with desire. "I've got to go now, Aunt Jane."

"Okay," said his aunt. "But I want the whole story before the end of the week!"

"Yes, ma'am. 'Bye, now."

He grabbed the chopstick and threw it away. Then he tussled with Dixie for a while after hanging up, but she was more interested in laughing than making love one more time.

"We can't, anyway," Flynn replied when she suggested she'd be willing if Flynn couldn't stand another hour without having her. He reached for the box on the bedside table and upturned it to show how empty the container was. "We're empty. I have to go to the drugstore."

She sat up with a sigh. "Well, I have to go to the theater today, anyway. It's about time we got dressed."

"We don't have to do that yet," Flynn said, coaxing her back among the pillows. He couldn't get enough of her. Just seeing her in his bed was exciting enough. "Can't I just look at you?"

She touched him intimately. "I think you have more than looking in mind."

"No, really, I just— Oh, Dixie."

She disappeared under the bedclothes and performed erotic magic. Flynn let her have her way with him until he was a crazy animal.

Later, while he regained his strength, she sat naked beside him and telephoned one of her theater friends. She asked Kiki if she'd stop by the Plaza and pick up a few things from her suite.

"I'll be happy to," Kiki had replied when all the arrangements were settled. "But have you seen the papers?"

Kiki reported that the New York newspapers had all picked up the story of the infamous Texas Tornado dumping her mobster boyfriend for a wealthy California boxer.

"Kiki says the photos of you are pretty good," Dixie said when she hung up. "You look rich and menacing. I guess you're a better actor than you think."

They bought newspapers on the way to the theater in the late afternoon, and read every printed lie in Dixie's dressing room. All of Dixie's friends stopped to hang out, and some of the actors offered Flynn advice about his role as they scanned the tabloids. Everyone seemed delighted that Dixie's plan appeared to be working. He was glad to see her so well liked and appreciated by her friends.

Even the theater's hairdresser stopped by to give him a trim. She wielded her scissors expertly, saying around a mouthful of bubble gum, "Just a little off the sides, see? And you'll look even more dangerous, know what I mean?"

Flynn didn't see it, but he allowed her to do whatever she pleased.

Kiki, who had been reading while perched on Dixie's dressing table, suddenly flapped her newspaper to get everyone's attention. "Hey, you guys! This reporter says the cops are looking into Joey Torrano, too."

"What for?" someone asked, laughing. "Which one of his crimes, I mean? He's done practically everything that's illegal in the state, so if— Oh, sorry, Dixie."

Dixie shook her head. "I never claimed he was a saint."

"Still," Kiki said, looking worried, "if he goes to jail before he gives us the money we need, we could be in real trouble."

"I think he's safe from the police," Dixie said confidently.

Keeping his silence, Flynn watched Dixie. She seemed very sure of Joey Torrano's innocence. But how did she really feel about the man she'd almost married? Protective? Would she be furious when she discovered that he was one of the cops looking to put Torrano away?

He shifted uncomfortably. He didn't like lying to her, but he still intended to get Torrano arrested as soon as possible. With a pang, Flynn realized the arrest might ruin everything Dixie had planned in order to save *The Flatfoot and the Floozie*.

"Hold still," the hairdresser lectured when he gave an involuntary wince. "You don't want a big bald spot over here, do you?"

"Sorry."

Sitting very still, Flynn fought down a rush of dread inside.

What if his role in Torrano's arrest blew everything with Dixie? Knowing her impulsive nature, she might fly off the handle. She might never forgive Flynn for his actions.

Flynn sat under the hairdresser's scissors and watched Dixie while she laughed with her friends. His heart gave an awful jerk.

At last all the other actors scattered to their respective dressing rooms, and Dixie began her preshow warm-up ritual. Rather than watch her massage at the hands of Sven, Flynn told her he had errands to run.

He kissed her quickly and slipped away, aware he had police work to do after days of making love to the

woman he was supposed to be keeping under surveillance—the woman he was supposed to be using.

As he left, Flynn promised himself to find a way to
tell Dixie he wasn't really a bike mechanic. She had a
right to know the truth about him. Before he de-
stroyed all her dreams.

Tuesday's show went well for Dixie. She felt refreshed and in full voice. Her high spirits after the show
made for a volatile night in Flynn's bed. On Wednesday, she played the afternoon matinee and the evening
performance, too, and went back to Flynn's apartment exhausted.

"Want to go across the street and get a bite to eat?"
Flynn asked, after being strangely silent all day. "It's
quiet over there. We could...talk about a few things."

"What do you want to talk about?"

He shrugged. "Whatever."

Dixie yawned and stretched her sore muscles.
Wednesdays were hard on her, with the two performances. "I don't think I have the energy. Maybe I'll
just have a bowl of cereal and go to bed."

"Okay."

She hooked her thumbs through Flynn's belt loops
and pulled him close. "Want to come with me?"

Flynn smiled and finally wrapped his arms around
her. "Do I get to choose the cereal?"

"Choose your pleasure," she invited, lifting her
mouth to be kissed.

On Thursday Dixie slept late and woke up alone in the apartment. Flynn had left a note on the bathroom mirror.

"Be back around two."

Dixie checked the time and found it was barely after noon.

The time had come, she decided, to make things happen with Joey. She knew she'd better ask for the money to support the show soon—while he was still riled up enough to fall for her plan.

She made a phone call. The number was one she'd memorized.

When a gruff voice picked up the line, she said, "I want to speak to Joey. It's Dixie."

The voice laughed harshly. "Who says he wants to talk to you?"

"Just put him on, George." Dixie knew Joey's chief bodyguard well. He was an unpleasant person, all right. The last time she'd seen him, he'd been sprawled on the sidewalk outside the church. Judging by his voice, George wasn't prepared to forget that incident.

"Call back another time," George snapped. "Like next year, when you're a has-been."

"If Joey hears I called and you kept us from talking, who's going to be a has-been, George?"

For an instant there was no answer. Then he said, "I'll ask."

Nearly five minutes went by, but Dixie was prepared to wait. Finally Joey's voice came over the line.

"What do you want?"

Joey's temper was already riled, but Dixie had thought long and hard about her pitch. She had consulted all her friends and written a script carefully.

Keeping her composure, she began, "Joey, honey, I want you to know the papers are printing a bunch of lies."

"You expect me to believe that? I got pictures of the guy you're with!" He was breathing hard already.

"It was a passing thing, Joey." She feigned an emotional crack in her voice. "I—I need to see you again."

"What for?"

"Just let me see you, Joey. I'd like to talk."

"I got no time for you!"

"Joey, please."

Dixie expected to beg. She knew Joey's ego would demand certain behavior from her, and she was prepared to give him his money's worth. So she wheedled shamelessly. It was part of the plan.

At last Joey said, "Okay, come on up to my place."

"I can't come there. The photographers are always waiting around. Let's meet someplace else."

"You got any ideas?"

"Central Park?"

He laughed. "You think you're gonna keep this meeting a secret if we hold it in Central Park?"

"I won't be all dolled up."

Joey said, "Okay. At this address. Ask a cabdriver to drop you. Unless you're coming with the boxer—"

"I'll be alone. What's the address?"

He gave Dixie a location in Central Park. She wrote it down to make sure she got it right. "In an hour, Joey?"

"Yeah, okay."

"One more thing. Make sure nobody's following you."

"I'll bust their cameras if they do."

"I don't mean photographers, Joey."

"What are you talkin' about—cops? Don't make me laugh!"

Then Joey hung up without saying goodbye.

Dixie took a fast shower and dressed in some of the clothes her friend had managed to sneak out of the Plaza—a pair of leggings and a shapeless gray shirt that didn't do much for her figure. Then she looked at her hair and decided she needed a hat.

Maybe Flynn had one.

She opened his closet and began rummaging around in his sports equipment. Sure enough, a navy blue baseball-style cap lay between a softball glove and bat. She picked it up.

"N.Y.P.D." She read the letters aloud.

"What in tarnation?"

Why would Flynn have a cop's hat? Dixie shrugged. She'd ask him later. Jamming the hat over her short hair, Dixie took a look in the mirror and liked the way it hid her hair and shaded her face. She scribbled Flynn a quick note telling him she would meet him later at the theater.

Then she phoned Jerry, her favorite cabdriver. He picked her up within half an hour at the corner.

Central Park was relatively busy—full of people having lunch outdoors on a warm day. Dixie had counted on being in public view, so she was glad to have a few honest citizens around. She waited at the agreed-upon entrance to the park, trying to be inconspicuous. Without her Dixie Davis getup, hardly anyone glanced her way.

For once she felt like Diana Davis, ordinary citizen.

At last a dark gray sedan pulled up at the curb. There was nothing special about the car—which made it special to Dixie. She wasn't surprised when Joey stepped out of the back, followed by George, the Neanderthal bodyguard. She was glad to see his swollen black eye.

George hung back, but obviously intended to tag along.

Joey, dressed in a comfortable jogging suit that concealed the paunch around his belly, advanced on Dixie swiftly. He had a quick way of moving, always had. He took Dixie's arm without a word and guided her into the park.

"Hiya, honey."

"You can walk with me," he said shortly, in spite of her friendly greeting. "I need the exercise."

Joey wasn't a tall man—barely Dixie's height, in fact, and he tried to keep in relatively good shape. He walked daily and drank very little. His passion, however, was pasta and spicy food, so fighting his weight was a constant battle. He was attractive, though, with strong features, dark hair that was trimmed weekly and a protruding lower lip that gave him a sulky expression some women found attractive. Dixie had begun to find it annoying.

"You look good," Dixie said, eager to please him. "Really good, honey."

"What do you care?"

"You know I care, Joey."

"Not enough," he retorted. "You humiliated me. Nobody does that and gets away with it."

"You got a lot of good publicity, though," Dixie ventured, keeping up with his brisk pace as they headed down one of the paved paths.

Joey didn't answer.

"Maybe people read the papers and figured I was a bitch for leaving you the way I did. Maybe people like you better now," she suggested. "I think maybe it was a good thing for your image, you know?"

Joey kept walking, silent. Dixie must have given him some food for thought, because he eventually said, "I didn't think of it that way."

"Well, it's what a few people were saying around the theater."

Joey's pace slackened slightly. "Yeah?"

"I didn't exactly make any new friends acting the way I did."

"So, people like me at the theater now?"

"They always liked you, Joey. You're a charismatic guy."

Dixie buttered him up some more, filling Joey Torrano's already swelled head with an improved idea of himself. She almost managed to have him believing that she was the villain in the story for jilting him at the altar. Joey's mood improved, and she happily realized that the first part of her plan had worked.

"Let's sit down, do you mind?" Dixie asked at last. "I can't keep up with you."

She was hardly out of breath, but she pretended to need a rest so she could watch Joey's face more closely. She had baited the hook, and now she intended to sink it deep.

Joey steered her toward a bench that overlooked the pond where a dozen or so children and adults appeared to be sailing model boats. A group of teenagers nearby played a portable CD player and swirled around it on in-line skates. A middle-aged woman on the next bench was reading a paperback book and eating a green apple.

"Okay," Joey said, getting comfortable on the bench. "What did you want to see me about?"

Dixie hesitated. "To apologize, first of all. I'm sorry about what happened to us, Joey. It's all my fault. I know you'll never take me back after the way I've hurt you, but—I just wanted you to know that I respect the way you've handled the mess I caused."

It was the right speech to make. It polished Joey's self-esteem while taking all the blame and also vetoing the possibility of getting back together. Joey seemed to like the words, so Dixie kept going—rephrasing things over and over until he was nodding and patting her hand.

Maybe Dixie was a better actress than she'd first thought. A few lessons and some weeks practicing the craft on a Broadway stage had certainly improved her ability to tell whopping lies. Joey seemed to believe everything she was saying.

Cautiously, she moved to the next step in her plan.

"I think I'm most sorry about ruining your investment," she said.

"What investment?"

"In *The Flatfoot and the Floozie.* I know how much you enjoyed producing your first Broadway show, and I—well, I wish I hadn't spoiled things for you."

"I'm still the producer."

"Yes, but—well, your initial contract is up. Since we've only been running a couple of weeks, we haven't turned a profit yet. The show will have to close."

"Um," said Joey, noncommittally.

"Your investment will be down the drain, and it's all my fault."

"Well..."

"I guess there's a chance this boxer from California will jump into the show, but he's—well, he's just not you, Joey. He doesn't understand show business the way you do. You have such a natural instinct—"

"I've always followed show business," he murmured. "It was kind of a hobby for me."

"Hobby!" Dixie manufactured a laugh. "I wish I had a hobby that was so profitable!"

"I haven't made a cent. Not yet."

"Well, you could have with *Flatfoot*. If I hadn't botched things up, that is. I'm sure your next show will be a hit."

Dixie sighed and waited. It was up to Joey to suggest the next move.

Joey thought things over. He wasn't the kind of man to make decisions quickly. The reason he had avoided getting caught by the police was his unwillingness to jump into any deal without carefully examining all the angles.

At last he said, "Maybe we ought to meet again, Dixie. Over dinner."

"Dinner?"

He looked at her. His eyes were flat and colorless in a face that was otherwise quite handsome. Dixie had been unnerved by those eyes the first time she'd met him, and she still found herself shivering as she looked into them. Joey was not a man to take lightly. She reminded herself that many people close to Joey had disappeared under mysterious circumstances.

Joey said, "Yeah, dinner. Nothing romantic. Just— we could talk a little business."

"I'm no good at business, Joey—"

"About *The Flatfoot and the Floozie*. I'm not a man who backs out on deals, you know."

"Well, not usually, but this time you've certainly got reason—"

"And I don't like getting muscled by some guy who thinks he's tough just because he bloodied a few noses in a boxing ring."

Dixie saw Joey's face turn red, and she tried to smooth his ruffled feathers. "Nobody ever said—"

"So let's get together," Joey went on. "Tonight after the show."

"Tonight?"

"Yeah. You got a problem with that?"

"No, no problem. Can we go to your place in Brooklyn?"

He smiled coldly. "You like my new restaurant?"

"I love Mexican food. You know that."

"Okay. Meet me there after the show. I'll send a car."

"Thanks, Joey." Dixie leaned over and kissed his cheek. She squeezed his hand, too. "You're a wonderful man, Joey Torrano."

"Yeah," he said with another smile. "I know."

Dixie left him in the park. As she departed, she couldn't help glancing back. Joey waved.

And the woman who'd been reading a paperback on the opposite bench looked up, too. She was wearing sunglasses and had a shoulder bag at her side. For some reason, Dixie noticed an extra strap.

As she turned to go, Dixie realized the extra strap belonged to a pistol harness.

The woman reading the book was a cop.

Dixie hurried up the path and caught a cab on the street. She gave the address of the theater and sat back in the seat, wondering if everything was going to fall apart before she finished the job of snowing Joey Torrano into financing *The Flatfoot and the Floozie.*

"God, I hope not," she murmured out loud.

At the weekly meeting of Sergeant Kello's Organized Crime Unit that afternoon, Flynn couldn't believe his ears.

"She did *what?*"

Detective Lucy Belsano glanced up from her notes. "I observed them in the park for twenty minutes, Flynn. Whatever the Davis woman is up to, it definitely includes our man Torrano."

"That's impossible." Flynn controlled the urge to say more. Already his colleagues were looking at him curiously. They didn't need to know he'd developed quite an unprofessional relationship with the woman they were currently discussing.

"Evidently, it's not completely impossible," Kello remarked, glancing at Flynn over the tops of his glasses.

"If you don't mind me saying so," Detective Belsano went on, "I think we should look into this Davis babe more carefully. I mean, she's from Texas, right? That's the state right beside Mexico, y'know. Maybe she's more involved than we first thought."

Flynn fought down the protests that rose instinctively in him and managed to say quite calmly, "Sergeant, did you talk to your friend at Immigration?"

"She's been busy," Kello reported. "Something big is happening over there, so she said she'd get back to me in a day or two. Until then, we've got to go with what we've got. Can we arrest Torrano on the racketeering charge?'

"The D.A.'s office says it's not a clean-cut case, but it's as good as anything else at the moment.''

Kello frowned for a long moment. Then he nodded. "Let's do it.''

"Arrest him?" Flynn questioned, suddenly worried. "Are you sure that's smart? I mean, if we wait a couple more days—''

"What's the matter, Flynn? I thought you wanted to bust the guy as much as the rest of us.''

"Of course I do, but—''

Kello waved off further discussion. "Pick up Torrano.''

Belsano stood eagerly. "Now?''

"Tonight. That way the D.A. will have an extra day to get their ducks in order.''

Belsano nodded. "Sounds good. Who's coming along on the bust?''

"Hell," said Kello with a grin. "We've been breaking our buns on this one. Why not take the whole damn department?''

Everyone cheered as the meeting broke up. Except for Flynn.

*It's too soon,* he thought. *I need to know how Dixie fits into all this. And how I'm going to get her out of it.*

# Nine

Flynn arrived at the theater later than he'd intended. He entered Dixie's dressing room and found it empty.

Kiki Barnes flew in after him, wide-eyed and frightened. She struggled with the zipper on her costume. "Flynn! Thank heaven! Where's Dixie?"

"Isn't she here?" Flynn automatically zipped the dress she was wearing.

Kiki shook her head wildly. "Dixie never showed up. Where is she?"

"I haven't seen her since this morning."

"Then where—" Kiki covered her mouth with both hands as if to stifle a scream. "Oh, Flynn, the curtain goes up in fifteen minutes! Where could she be?"

Flynn cursed. He felt the blood leave his face, and a dizzying wave of fear overtook him.

"Oh, God," Kiki breathed, staring at him. "Something terrible's happened, hasn't it? Joey did something, didn't he?"

Flynn grabbed Kiki by her arms. "Don't panic," he ordered, forcing her to pull herself together. "Maybe Dixie just got stranded somewhere. You know her. Maybe she got an urge to see the Statue of Liberty."

Even he didn't believe that story.

"But what about the... the show?"

"You'll have to figure something out." Flynn let her go. "In the meantime, I'll find Dixie."

"Flynn, please be careful. Joey is—he's not a nice man."

"Tell me about it," Flynn growled.

Dixie should have known something was wrong as soon as Jerry, her cabdriver, took a wrong turn just a block from the Plaza. But it wasn't until he had taken her miles in the wrong direction that she figured out there was something definitely bad happening. The biggest tip-off was that Jerry wasn't his usual talkative self.

"Jerry, what's going on?" She sat forward on the cab's bouncing seat.

Jerry was sweating, but he kept both hands firmly on the wheel of the car and his eyes fixed on the road. "I'm sorry, Miss Davis. I'm really sorry."

"It's Joey, isn't it?"

Jerry dashed perspiration from his forehead. "He's my boss, Miss Davis. I have to do what he tells me."

"I've got a show to do tonight, Jerry. The theater is sold-out—"

"I'm sorry. I'm really sorry."

"Can you at least tell me where we're going?"

"Mr. Torrano said to bring you. He didn't say anything about talking to you."

Dixie sat back in her seat, annoyed and just a little scared. She should have guessed Joey had something up his sleeve. He had been too agreeable in the park. Of course he wasn't going to give her what she wanted—not without punishing her first.

Dixie swallowed hard. What did Joey have in mind?

Flynn called Belsano from a pay phone outside the theater. "You're in charge of tonight's detail, right?"

"Right," she said, a tough cop who was always suspicious. "What's it to you?"

"I need to know—is there a tail on Torrano right now?"

"Yeah, sure. Why?"

"Can you tell me where he is?"

"In a car headed across the Brooklyn Bridge, last time I heard. Why?"

"Thanks, Belsano."

"Flynn, hold it. What are you—"

But Flynn had hung up. He climbed on the Harley and headed for Brooklyn as fast as the bike could go. His insides were tight with fear. Traffic was heavy, so he wove dangerously around the cars and trucks that blocked his way, and sped through traffic lights when he could. For once, he didn't care about his bike.

Dixie was in trouble. That's all that mattered.

Flynn parked his Harley on the street opposite a restaurant called Hacienda. He noticed a police sedan farther down the block and strode in that direction. Two of his buddies from Organized Crime were sitting in the car, both drinking diet 7Up from cans.

Flynn leaned in the driver's window. "Hey, Julio. What's going on?"

Julio Martinez nodded toward the restaurant. "We're keeping an eye on Joey Torrano until Belsano gets here to arrest him."

"Anybody in there with him?"

"The usual slime."

Flynn held on to his self-control. "A woman, by any chance?"

Julio and his partner laughed. "Why, Flynn? You looking for a date for once?"

"Just looking for someone. Dixie Davis."

"What—you lost her?" The two cops laughed some more. "Tough luck, Flynn."

"She didn't show up at the theater tonight."

Julio's expression changed. "You think Torrano snatched her?"

Flynn was afraid to answer. He glanced up and down the block, hoping to catch a glimpse of Dixie and taking a second to control the panic he felt rising inside.

Julio leaned out the window. "Hey, Flynn, take it easy, man. You need some help?"

"Yeah. I think we'd better not wait for Belsano."

"You mean, we go arrest Torrano now? Just us?" Julio blinked, startled. "Without a warrant?"

"Call Belsano on the radio. She must be on her way pretty soon. We can stall until she gets here. Come on, Julio. Dixie might be in trouble."

Dixie was dropped off at the back of Joey's restaurant. Her driver, Jerry, apologized again. Then George escorted Dixie inside the kitchen of the restaurant.

Dixie had a bad feeling about the whole operation. She felt her knees shaking as she remembered the tales she'd heard about some of Joey's dealings with employees who had served out their usefulness.

She checked her watch. Almost curtain time at the theater.

None of the kitchen workers looked up from their job as Dixie entered. In fact, they barely looked at each other. The kitchen was eerily quiet except for the salsa music playing on the radio over near the dishwasher.

George hustled Dixie through a swinging door, and she found herself in the dim dining room of Joey's Mexican restaurant. The room was very dark, but she could make out a few tacky fiesta-type decorations on the walls and hanging from the ceiling. Perhaps twenty patrons were eating. A single waiter hurried worriedly from table to table. He didn't look too happy to be the only one on duty—or about wearing a gigantic sombrero.

Steam rose in clouds from the buffet table, but the food didn't smell too authentic to Dixie, who knew her way around Tex-Mex food very well indeed.

Joey sat alone at a round table in one corner. He had a drink in front of him, along with several plates of spicy Mexican food he'd chosen from the buffet. He appeared to be taking some tablets for an upset stomach.

Dixie made an effort to look cheerful as she approached the table. "Hiya, Joey, honey. What a surprise! I thought we were having dinner after the show."

"Sit down," Joey said, wiping his lips with a napkin and putting his bottle of tablets back into a coat pocket. He jerked his head at George, indicating the bodyguard should leave them alone. George disappeared.

Dixie eased into the chair beside Joey's. "Honey, the food smells delicious."

But Joey cut across her words, saying, "It smells like garbage and tastes a lot worse. Whose idea was it to open a Mexican restaurant in a Jewish neighborhood in Brooklyn, anyway?"

Dixie didn't point out that it was his idea. Instead she said, "Listen, Joey, if we could just—"

"Just shut up and listen."

"But—"

He silenced her with a deadly look. Then he said slowly, "I hate to do this to you, Dix."

* * *

"Absolutely not," Belsano screamed into the radio. "Don't arrest Torrano until I get there, Flynn! Don't do it! I haven't got the warrant yet! The judge won't listen to me. Don't you dare—"

Flynn terminated the call. "Let's go," he said to Julio. "I feel hungry."

The three cops crossed the street together. Then Julio cut around the back of the restaurant with the intention of entering through the kitchen door. Flynn and the other cop waited two minutes, then pushed through the front door. It took a few moments for their eyes to become accustomed to the gloom. Julio came out of the kitchen a second later.

Then Flynn saw Dixie and his heart almost stopped.

She sat, white faced, in front of Joey Torrano, who didn't look happy.

Flynn took a breath and approached the table, flanked by the other two cops.

Joey looked up and glared. Dixie looked up and blanched with fear. Her blue eyes were saucer-size.

"Joey Torrano," Flynn said firmly. "You're under arrest."

"Go to hell," said Torrano. "You ain't got nothing on me. I talked to the judge myself."

"You have the right to remain silent," Flynn continued, Torrano's words not registering in his brain.

"Where's your warrant? What's the charge?"

"Anything you say can be held against you in a court of law—"

*"What's the charge?"*

"Oh, God," said Dixie. "This can't be happening. Flynn—what in the world are you *doing?*"

Julio circled the table and took out his handcuffs.

Flynn gave up trying to remember the rights speech. He said, "Dixie, I'm sorry. I should have told you before. I'm a cop."

"A *cop?*" She leapt to her feet so suddenly that her chair fell over.

"I kept it a secret because I knew—"

"You're a *cop?*" she shrieked, slamming both hands down onto the table so hard the silverware jumped. Her glare began to throw sparks. "I can't believe you'd do this!"

Flynn's heart sank and he tried to reach for her hand. "I know this is bad, but—"

She jerked her hand away. "Of all the colossal nerve!"

Joey Torrano began to shout, too. Then Julio raised his voice to continue reciting, "You have the right to remain silent." Suddenly everyone was yelling.

"Of all the low-down tricks!"

"I should have told you, but I never found the right time!"

"You can't arrest me without a warrant!"

"An attorney will be provided for you—"

The noise was incredible. Suddenly Dixie grabbed one of the plates of food in front of Torrano. She picked it up and hurled it directly at Flynn. A flurry of stale taco chips hit Flynn directly in the chest, silencing everyone.

As every person in the room froze, Dixie roared, "I demand that you tell me *everything* this minute!"

"Dixie—"

He had no intention of stalling, but his momentary hesitation fueled a fury like no other Flynn had ever seen. Enraged, Dixie grabbed another plate—this one full of diced tomatoes and guacamole. She heaved it, but Flynn had the wits to duck in time.

The plate sailed over his head and hit George instead as the bodyguard was coming across the restaurant floor like a bull headed for a red flag. The guacamole splattered all over the front of George's shirt, looking as if he'd been brutally shot and was leaking green blood.

A woman dining at a nearby table screamed.

Julio gave up trying to arrest Torrano and made a futile grab for Dixie's throwing arm.

But Dixie faked him out and grabbed another plate with her left hand, then succeeded in splatting it directly into Julio's immaculate white shirt.

"Why, you little—" Julio grabbed a smeary handful of the Mexican food on his chest and threw it at Dixie's face.

She reacted by hurling the last plate, which missed Julio by a mile and smacked Joey Torrano in the chin. Joey roared and threw it back at her, hitting Julio instead.

Then the fight was on. Julio backed up and took a defensive position beside the buffet table, where he could grab bowls of soupy sauces and heave them at anyone who moved. His partner slipped in the mess on the carpet and fell heavily, cursing. He grabbed a tablecloth on the way down and yanked an entire tableful of food down upon himself. The patrons at the table screamed and fled.

Except for the teenage son, who yelled, "Food fight!" And he joined the battle.

George fought his way to his knees and began scraping food off the floor and throwing it at Flynn. He hit Dixie squarely in the face with a handful of guacamole instead. He laughed. She reacted at once, fury on her brow, by grabbing an entire tray of dirty dishes from a nearby table and heaving it with all her strength. The crash was incredible. George bolted for cover.

Flynn stood helplessly in the middle of the fray. "What the hell did I do wrong?" he asked rhetorically.

"What did you do wrong?" Dixie cried, staggering drunkenly under an onslaught of flying food. "What did you do *wrong*?"

Flynn tried to defend himself. "Dixie, I never meant things to go this far, but—"

He was cut off by a sailing glob of cold enchilada that struck him flat on the cheek.

Dixie burst out laughing. "Serves you right!"

Flynn felt his temper blow like a tire on the freeway. He fell back like a quarterback evading tough linemen and found himself standing by the dessert bar. He grabbed a bowl of whipped cream and threw it at Dixie.

"Serves *me* right?" he shouted as the white cream exploded on her chest. "Just what the hell are you doing here and why couldn't you have the decency to tell me what's going on? And what *is* going on, by the way?"

Dixie didn't have a chance to answer. She ducked a flying plate of assorted salad items thrown by the teenager and lost her footing in the whipped cream on the floor. She fell down within the melee.

Flynn dived to rescue her. Too late. She was already sitting up and managed to throw whipped cream into his face as he arrived beside her. She burst out laughing again.

Grimly, Flynn dragged her under a table for safety.

"Now," he said, pinning her to the floor. "What's going on?"

She was still laughing. "Did I ever tell you how great you look in whipped cream?"

Even covered with food, she looked gorgeous. Flynn's chest expanded at the sight of her, and the relief that swelled inside him was enormous. She was safe. She was in his arms. And she was laughing.

He said, "I love you."

"I know," she replied, looping her arms around his neck. "I love you, too."

Her kiss was just as powerful then as it had been the moment she'd first fastened her delicious lips to Flynn's. Except this time she tasted of whipped cream in addition to sex, laughter and high spirits. Flynn groaned with pleasure and gathered her completely into his arms.

And that was the way Sergeant Kello and the rest of the Organized Crime Unit found them ages later—locked in each other's embrace and murmuring sweet nothings between powerfully good kisses.

"What the hell," Kello demanded, "is going on here?"

His thundering voice—along with eight uniformed cops—managed to bring the food fight to a standstill.

When things had quieted down, Flynn crawled out from under the table. "Uh, hello, Sergeant."

"Flynn—"

Then Dixie sat up. She pulled off her food-strewn N.Y.P.D. baseball cap and fluffed her short blond hair.

"*Davis?*" Kello demanded. "Is that you?"

Flynn was puzzled. "How do you two know each other?"

Kello snapped, "Never mind that now! What's going on? Where's Torrano?"

Julio dragged Joey Torrano up out of a mess of dirty dishes on the floor. "Here, sir."

"What are you doing with him?"

Julio said, "Making an arrest, sir."

"With what? We haven't got a warrant!"

Flynn groaned. The rest of the cops looked devastated. Months of hard investigative work had just gone down the tubes. Kello glared furiously at Flynn.

Dixie climbed to her feet. "I guess it's up to me, then."

"What?" Flynn clambered up beside her. "What are you talking about?"

From inside a pocket of her gray shirt, Dixie withdrew a thin leather wallet and flipped it open. Inside, for all to see, was a police shield.

She smiled wanly at Flynn, then turned to Joey Torrano.

"Mr. Torrano," she said. "You're under arrest for violations of the United States' Code of Immigrations. I have a warrant for your arrest and extradition papers to the State of Texas for importing illegal aliens into this country."

"You're a *cop?*" Flynn demanded.

"Wait a minute," Kello interrupted. "How do you know Detective Davis?"

"*Detective?* Are you kidding? This is *her!* This is Dixie Davis, the Texas Tornado!"

"Just for a few weeks," Dixie explained, looking just a little sheepish for keeping secrets. "The rest of the time, I'm an immigration officer. I'm in New York on special assignment to see that Joey Torrano is put behind bars."

Together, Kello and Flynn said, "I don't believe this."

# Epilogue

They adjourned to the Plaza Hotel later, for a hot bath and room service.

"You could have told me," Flynn said gruffly.

"You could have told *me*," she corrected. "I thought you were a motorcycle mechanic!"

"But you had me believing you were a Broadway star!"

They relaxed in the bathtub together, surrounded by mountains of perfumed bubbles. Dixie wore her trademark white hat, but Flynn was delightfully naked. She touched him under the water now and then to remind herself how wonderful he felt.

"I was a Broadway star," she said with a grin. "Can you believe it? I never imagined that part would happen. I came to New York to get close to Torrano, and an audition for his play seemed like a good way to get myself introduced.''

"And after all those years sitting at the knee of your granny Butterfield, you knew a thing or two about being a showgirl."

"Right. I guess I wasn't bad, but flirting with Torrano got me elevated to star status. Then I had to cover my real identity so nobody would tip off Joey to my real job.''

"So you invented the Texas Tornado.''

"Yep. You can't imagine how many frantic phone calls I made to Mama for advice.''

"Apparently," Flynn murmured, nuzzling her moist neck, "her advice was very good.''

Her nerve endings tingled with delight. "O-oh, Flynn. Don't start something you can't finish.''

"Who says I can't finish? I may be shell-shocked after tonight's events, but nothing will keep me out of your bed this evening, Miss Tornado.''

Dixie sighed and let him gather her body close. "I'm glad you came along tonight, you know.''

He stopped kissing her earlobes and looked solemnly into her eyes. "Are you?''

"Of course! I wasn't sure I could handle Torrano myself.''

"But . . .'' He hesitated. "I'm sorry about *The Flatfoot and the Floozie.* You were serious about keeping the show going, weren't you?''

"Absolutely.''

"Now what's going to happen?" Flynn asked. "With Torrano in jail, his bank accounts will be frozen. All contracts will be canceled."

Dixie smiled wickedly. "I thought of that."

"You did?"

Dixie pulled loose from Flynn's embrace and slid over to the side of the huge tub. She reached over the edge and groped on the floor for her shirt. Dripping water, she carefully extracted a small rectangle of paper.

"What's that?"

"A cashier's check," Dixie answered, holding it up to the light. She reclined beside Flynn and smiled up at her prize. "It's for half-a-million dollars—enough to keep the show going long enough to find another investor, I think."

"But how did—"

"I sweet-talked Torrano into writing me a check before you showed up tonight. After he fired me from the show."

"He *fired* you?"

"As a punishment for making him look foolish. He says Kiki can take over my role."

"She had her crack at it tonight," Flynn said, then explained his rushed conversation with Kiki before the show that night.

"I hope she pulled it off," Dixie said. "I'll call her in the morning. She'll want to hear the news about the check, too."

He grinned and removed her hat, tossing it aside. "Not this minute."

She cast the check onto the nearby counter and glided back into Flynn's arms with a contented sigh.

As his embrace closed around her, Dixie was suddenly overwhelmed by how lucky she was. She'd done her job under almost impossible circumstances. She'd managed to fulfill a lifelong fantasy by singing and dancing on the kind of stage her mother and grandmother had been on before her.

But most of all, she'd found love. The kind of love Dixie had long ago decided wasn't possible for her. She'd found Flynn—strong, funny, impulsive when he needed to be, steady as a rock when the situation called for it.

"I do love you," she said, tracing a pattern of bubbles on his chest.

"I'm glad," he said huskily. "And I love you, Diana Davis, or whoever you are. But now what happens?"

"We spend a wonderful night together?"

"A last night?" he asked, sounding tense.

"I—I hope not."

With one finger on her chin, Flynn turned Dixie's face to his. He found her lips with his gently. She opened her mouth and tried to tease his tongue with her own, but Flynn wasn't in a teasing mood. He deepened the kiss and tightened his arms around her.

Dixie felt his body come alive, pressed to hers. Her own began to tremble with desire. "Flynn—"

"I want you," he murmured. "So badly. Now and forever."

"Now and forever," she whispered back, holding on tight and fighting absurd tears.

He pulled Dixie out of the tub and carried her—wet and lithe—into the bedroom. The huge bed absorbed the water as they rolled together, suddenly feverish in their passion. It felt so good to be with him, so right.

Dixie held on tight as Flynn caressed each square inch of her skin as if trying to remember its texture for a long time.

She had to choke back a cry as he found his way inside her quickly. He sank deeply, as if claiming Dixie's body for his own. Then they rocked together until the melding of flesh became the melding of spirits. A bright flame burst between them, hot and powerful. Dixie feared she might fall off the edge of the earth, but Flynn was there to catch her.

"I love you."

The words seemed to beat along with their hearts.

Along toward morning, when the sunlight was just starting to lighten Central Park, Dixie felt strong enough to talk.

She rolled against Flynn's side and put her head on his shoulder. "Flynn, I don't belong in New York."

"I know," he said, still awake, too. He sounded calm.

"My life and my family—everything's in Texas. Here, I'm a freak, an alien."

"You're not."

"I am. It feels wrong for me here. Except for you."

"All right," he said, quieting her with gentle pressure on her hand as it lay just above his beating heart. "Then I guess it's up to me, isn't it?"

Dixie lifted her head to look at him. "What do you mean?"

In the half-light that gleamed down on a quiet New York City, Flynn's smile shone slightly. "Is there room in Texas for an Irish cop?"

"But, Flynn, your family! Your brother, Aunt Jane—everything! You'd give that up?"

"I have to," he said. "I can't be without you, Diana."

She sighed. "Thank heavens. I thought I was going to have to use the Butterfield kiss again."

His laugh was deep and incredulous, and she loved the dark look he cast down at her. "The what?"

"It's—well, maybe you'd better not know." Wisely, Dixie decided to keep that secret a little longer. She patted his chest to placate him. "Once we're married, I may need to use it now and then."

"Married, huh? Can we do that on the way to Texas?"

"On the way?"

"Sure. I thought we'd take the Harley."

"The whole way on a motorcycle?"

"Not just a motorcycle. It's a Harley."

Dixie considered the idea, smiling. "It will be a nice, long trip, won't it?"

"We'll make it last a lifetime, if that's what you want."

Dixie snuggled down with him again. "It's definitely what I want, Flynn."

*     *     *     *     *

# DREAM WEDDING
## by Pamela Macaluso

Don't miss JUST MARRIED, a fun-filled series by Pamela Macaluso about three men with wealth, power and looks to die for. These bad boys had everything—except the love of a good woman.

\*\*\*

"What a nerd!" Those taunting words played over and over in Alex Dalton's mind. Now that he was a rich, successful businessman—with looks to boot—he was going to make Genie Hill regret being so cruel to him in high school. All he had to do was seduce her…and then dump her. But could he do it without falling head over heels for her—again?

Find out in DREAM WEDDING, book two of the JUST MARRIED series, coming to you in May…only in

SILHOUETTE®

Desire®

JM1

# Take 4 bestselling love stories FREE

## Plus get a FREE surprise gift!

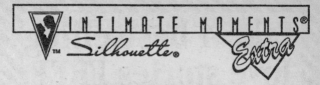

## CODE NAME: DANGER

*Because love is a risky business...*

Merline Lovelace's "Code Name: Danger" miniseries gets an explosive start in May 1995 with

### NIGHT OF THE JAGUAR, IM #637

Omega agent Jake MacKenzie had flirted with danger his entire career. But when unbelievably sexy Sarah Chandler became enmeshed in his latest mission, Jake knew that his days of courting trouble had taken a provocative twist....

Your mission: To read more about the Omega agency.

Your next target: THE COWBOY AND THE COSSACK, August 1995

Your only choice for nonstop excitement—

# COMING NEXT MONTH

**#931 SINGLE DAD—Jennifer Greene**

June's *Man of the Month*, Josh Penoyer, had no time for women
in his hectic life. But his kids wanted a new mom, and they'd
decided beautiful Ariel Lindstrom would be perfect for the job!

**#932 THE ENGAGEMENT PARTY—Barbara Boswell**

*Always a Bridesmaid!*
When Hannah Farley attended her friend's engagement party,
she never thought she could be the next one walking down the
aisle, *especially* with an arrogant yet sexy stranger named
Matthew Granger....

**#933 DR. DADDY—Liz Bevarly**

*From Here to Maternity*
Working with redhead Zoey Holland was more than Dr. Jonas Tate
could stand. But when he needed advice for raising his niece, he
found himself asking Zoey—and *wanting* the feisty woman....

**#934 ANNIE SAYS I DO—Carole Buck**

*Wedding Belles*
Annie Martin and Matt Powell had been inseparable friends since
they were kids. Now a "pretend" date had Matt wondering how to
get his independent and suddenly irresistible friend to say "I do!"

**#935 HESITANT HUSBAND—Jackie Merritt**

Mitch Conover refused to fall for his new boss's daughter, no
matter what the sexy woman made him feel. But Kim Armstrong
wouldn't give up until she worked her way into his heart....

**#936 RANCHER'S WIFE—Anne Marie Winston**

Angel Davis needed a vacation—not a headstrong rancher named
Day Ryder to boss her around. But it wasn't long before she fell
for his little girl...and the stubborn rancher *himself!*

## Announcing
# the New **Pages & Privileges**™ Program
### from Harlequin® and Silhouette®

## Get All This FREE
## With Just One Proof-of-Purchase!

- **FREE Travel Service** with the guaranteed lowest available airfares plus 5% cash back on every ticket

- **FREE Hotel Discounts** of up to 60% off at leading hotels in the U.S., Canada and Europe

- **FREE Petite Parfumerie** collection (a $50 Retail value)

- **FREE $25 Travel Voucher** to use on any ticket on any airline booked through our Travel Service

- **FREE Insider Tips Letter** full of fascinating information and hot sneak previews of upcoming books

- **FREE Mystery Gift** (if you enroll before May 31/95)

And there are more great gifts and benefits to come!
Enroll today and become Privileged!

(see insert for details)

---

 **PROOF-OF-PURCHASE**

Offer expires October 31, 1996                    SD-PP1